THE
CARNIVOROUS
CITY

THE CARNIVOROUS CITY

Toni Kan

Abuja – London

Toni Kan worked as a journalist for 5 years and rose to the position of editor at the age of 26 before moving into corporate Nigeria. Hailed as the 'Mayor of Lagos', Kan is the author of 4 critically acclaimed works of fiction and poetry. Winner of the NDDC/Ken Saro Wiwa literature prize (2009), awarded by the Association of Nigerian Authors, Kan is co–founder and publisher of sabinews.com and a fellow of the Heinrich Boll Stiftung, Civitella Ranieri and Yaddo.

Lagos is his playground.

First published in 2016 by Cassava Republic Press
Abuja – London

Copyright © Toni Kan, 2016

Nigerian ISBN 978-978-953-514-3
UK ISBN 978-1-911115-24-3
E-book ISBN 978-1-911115-25-0

A CIP catalogue record for this book is available from the National Library of Nigeria and British Library.

Book designed by Allan Milton Castillo Rivas.

Cover designed by Michael Salu.

Printed and bound in Great Britain by Bell & Bain Ltd, Glasgow.

Distributed in Nigeria by Book River Ltd.

Distributed in the UK by Central Books Ltd.

Stay up to date with the latest books, special offers
and exclusive content with our monthly newsletter.
Sign up on our website:
www.cassavarepublic.biz

Twitter: @cassavarepublic
Instagram: @cassavarepublicpress
Facebook: facebook.com/CassavaRepublic

Do you know, friend, how a brother loves his brother...
James Baldwin

SONI IS MISSING

Soni is missing.

Three simple words that seemed as if a lifetime had been compressed into them, a lethal payload of pain and fear waiting to detonate and decimate. Those words shocked and calmed in equal measure, like a letter bearing bad news delivered long after its contents have been made known.

That was the sum of the text message Abel received that morning and the one message he now had to forget. But there was a problem: to forget, you had to learn not to remember.

It was a Friday and he was sleeping in because the school where he taught English literature had gone on vacation a week before. With three free months ahead of him, Abel had decided to enjoy his sleep until he tired of it.

That was why his alarm did not go off at 5am as usual, and that was why, when his phone began to vibrate, he flung it across the room. The text came in at 5.43am, but he only read it at 6.05am, after he stepped on the handset as he exited the bathroom.

He sat on the chair by his reading table, naked save for his boxers, and looked at the message again.

Soni is missing.

It was short and direct; no frills.

His hands were shaking. He looked at his fingers as if he was seeing them for the first time: they were long and slender, the fingernails well-trimmed like a girl's. Calista, his ex-girlfriend, used to tease him.

They had been even slimmer and more girl-like when he was a sickly teenager. Things had changed after secondary school. He was still sickly but not as ill as he used to be. Then, because he began to lift weights and pump iron, his body had filled out. He would never be fat, but no one would now describe him as skinny or sickly.

Soni is missing.

The message had been sent for maximum impact and as he read it over and over again, he began to slowly admit to himself that, at some deep unconscious level, he had been expecting this message or a variant of it for years now.

Soni was his younger brother and someone who, in the peculiar speak of Lagos, had 'made it'. He was a bonafide 'Lagos Big Boy': a member of that amazing tribe of men who inhabited a social stratum of Lagos accessed mostly through shady deals or white-collar crime. They were the toast of musicians and the jet set but, like cheap goods in the Indian and Lebanese shops that dotted Lagos, they were always close to expiring.

Missing.

Shot.

Found dead.

On the run.

Declared wanted.

Arrested.

Detained.

These were words and phrases that usually preceded comments about those who had 'made it' in cities like Lagos.

No one could accuse Abel of being a Lagos Big Boy or mistake him for someone who had made it. As a teacher in a remote state capital, he subsisted on the basics. His needs were minimal. All the clothes he owned would fit into a small box. The only things he spent money on were the novels he ordered monthly from Jazzhole, through an old friend in Lagos.

On evenings when Abel did not wish to be buried in a novel or at the gym, he would go to Madam Caro's bar for a stout or two and shoot the breeze with the motley crew that gathered there: contractors, civil servants and their cohorts, politicians on the make. The topics were always the same: politics, money, football and sex.

Abel looked at the text message again. Even though it was not signed he knew who had sent it. There was no mistake about it. The message had come from Ada, Soni's wife and the mother of his three-year-old son. They had history between them, Ada and Abel.

He remembered when Soni had called to tell him about his plans to get married. Abel asked him who she was, where she was from and where they met. After Soni replied to say they had met in a nightclub, Abel wrote his younger brother a long letter that ended with, '9 inches, you do not marry a woman you met in a nightclub.'

And Soni, maybe in a fit of passion, had shown her the letter or maybe – not to judge him too harshly – had left it lying carelessly someplace like he did most things; clothes, money, memories. Ada had read those last lines and never forgot or forgave.

He called the number.

'Ada, it's me, Abel. I just got your message.'

'What message?' Her voice was flat.

'What message? Didn't you send me a text message?'

'No. I did not.'

'OK. Well, I got a message from this number to say Soni is missing. Is he?'

'Yes. He is missing.' Abel thought he heard a sniffle.

'And you didn't think to tell me?'

'I don't have your number,' she said, as if it was the perfect answer.

'You don't have my number?' Abel bit down on his lower lip to stop from screaming. He took a deep breath. 'How long has my brother been missing?'

'Sixteen days,' she said and burst into tears. 'I know you will blame me. I know you have never liked me.'

She was crying now and Abel hoped his phone credit would not run out of time.

'I wanted to call but I didn't know what to say. We are broke. We can't eat. I can't buy my son's cereal. The bank says I can't get money from his account because I am not his next of kin.'

'Who is his next of kin?' he asked, wondering why she would have kept the news from him for over two weeks.

'You are. All the money Soni has now belongs to you. Without you, we can't even buy toothpicks.' She burst into tears again.

That was when his credit ran out.

—

Soni had been born Sunderland Onyema Dike but over time he came to be known by an odd assortment of *noms de guerre* befitting the person he was becoming and would become.

At university he was known as '9 inches' because he told the girls he slept with that he was nine inches long and soon took to leaving an inscription on the wall above the bed of any girl he bedded: '9 inches was here'. And he bedded many girls.

It was a boast and a declaration all at once, aimed at deflating the next visitor.

After school, when he relocated to Lagos to 'chase his fortune', as he said, Soni came to be known first as Alhaji Tanko, then Sabato Jnr and finally Sabato Rabato.

Everyone said Soni had seen money. They said he had hit it big in Lagos. Having never made it in Lagos or anywhere else Abel did not have a firm understanding of what making it meant. He had caught glimpses of it during Soni's wedding to Ada. He gleaned it from the house Soni lived in previously, the gifts he scattered around the family, the magnificent house he built for their mum in the village, the brand new Toyota Camry he sent Abel on his thirty-fifth birthday, and the brand new cars he sent to their mum, their sister and a gaggle of uncles and aunties.

And he got a sense of it when he stepped into Soni's house in Lekki Phase 1, two days after he received Ada's text message.

Soni had built and moved into the house two years earlier. Abel had been invited to the house warming but could not make it because it fell during the second semester exams. He did not want to think about Soni's house, with its eight bedrooms and three living rooms, the fleet of seven cars, the wall-mounted flat-screen televisions and split-unit air conditioners in every space.

He focused his thoughts on Soni's son's room, which, in its sheer luxury, brought to the fore the shabbiness of his own digs and, in fact, his whole existence.

Wealth, luxury and opulence were not things he was familiar with. They had grown up the children of two teachers. He still had his memories from childhood, from when his father was a vice principal. They lived in the house on top of the knoll, where he would sit and watch his friends fit into the hollow of 32-inch rim tyres. They would scream and yell as the tyres raced downhill to the sand deposits where they were building new quarters. He was too sickly to join in.

Sometimes, the pusher would do something wrong and the tyres would miss the mounds of sand, go banging straight into the wall and the passenger would fall out bloodied.

Because Abel could not exert himself, he found refuge in the many books on his father's shelves. Books were easy. They did not require much effort. He could sit and read all day long then wake up and take a walk. You didn't get bruises, black eyes or missing teeth from reading books, and if your imagination was as fertile as his, you could travel great distances without leaving your doorstep.

Abel loved *Mine Boy* and *An African Night's Entertainment*. He loved Ben Okri and Ayi Kwei Armah. He liked Mariama Bâ's, *So Long a Letter*. As he grew older, his tastes became more American and then Indian writers began to appeal to him too.

Their family had lived on the school compound of St Patrick's College, where his father taught. For many years, it was a happy home with music and laughter. His father favoured jazz and blues, always playing records by artistes like Isaac Hayes, Hot Chocolate, Spiro Gyra and Earl Klugh.

His mother's taste was more sentimental. He still remembered her playing loud music on Saturday mornings as she and his sister did the chores, while his father was out playing tennis and Abel and Soni watched cartoons. She played Boney M. and ABBA if she was happy and Bob Marley's *No Woman, No Cry* if she was sad. The songs were the barometer of his mother's mood.

Abel still lived and worked in Asaba, a small town made slightly bigger by its newfound status as a state capital, especially with the annexation of Okpanam.

Okpanam was the home town of Chukwuma Kaduna Nzeogwu, Nigeria's first putschist, while Asaba was infamous as a theatre of war, where federal troops, led by Murtala Mohammed, allegedly called for a meeting of all adult men and gunned them down in cold blood.

Growing up, Abel did not know all this, but he remembered seeing fellow students at St Patrick's College dig up bones and skulls as they made ridges and hedges for agricultural science practicals.

Asaba was small then, its pretensions to town-hood circumscribed by the presence of only one road that deserved the name, Nnebisi

Road, which ran like an angry artery through the length of the town.

It was a sleepy place, with the only bustle evident at the Ogbeogonogo Market, and sometimes at Cable Point on your exit towards Onitsha Head Bridge, which led from Delta Igboland into the real Igbo hinterland.

This was where he grew up, where he had his first kiss and first shag and where, if Soni hadn't gone missing, he believed he would have expired.

Asaba held good memories but it was also a place of sadness, where his idyllic life changed on his twelfth birthday; the day he and his father came back home earlier than planned because someone had collapsed and died at the tennis court. They had found his mother in bed with the neighbour's kid brother; the one who had been sleeping with Abel's aunt.

Abel recalled his father shooing him away, willing him to go blind, to not see the sweaty entwined bodies lying on the matrimonial bed. Thankfully, his brother and sister were away at an aunt's for the weekend.

Abel remembered the boy, not much older than him, running off naked with his clothes under his armpits and his father falling to his knees, his tennis racquet in his hands. Abel stood there and watched, astonished at how naked and sexual his mother looked and ashamed at the stirring he felt.

He had seen her naked many times before, but that morning she looked different. Sweaty. Open. Those were the words that came to mind, and as he watched his father weep, he knew that his tears were not for what he had seen but on account of whom he had seen it with. Abel was an unwelcome spectator at his father's spectacle of shame and neither of them ever forgot it.

His father found solace in drink and the outdoors while his mother sought refuge in the church. But there was no comfort for Abel. He could not unsee what he had seen and he would never be able to talk about it. It was a secret he would bear to his grave, one that not only opened a wide gulf between him and his mother, but also told him clearly that he would never, ever get married.

—

From an early age, Abel knew what he wanted to be: a vice principal. Not a principal; just a vice principal like his father had been when the thought first occurred to the young Abel.

His father was the man he wanted to be: a teacher living a simple, idyllic life defined by certainties and the most basic rules. Wake. Warm the car. Go to work. Observe siesta. Drink a beer or two in the evening as you read a magazine or book. Play tennis on Wednesday nights and Saturday mornings.

His father had loved coffee and cigarettes. Abel remembered him smoking as they tried on clothes in the shops at Easter and Christmas.

Abel had resolved, right from when he was about nine or ten, that the only person he wanted to be like when he grew up was his father. But even though he had practised all his life for that wish, it did not come easily to him because by the time he was old enough to become his father, things had changed. Teaching had lost his allure and instead of respectability, it cloaked those who came to it in the garb of poverty and penury. He had embraced, with something close to physical ache, the realisation that, with the way things were going, he would never be able to afford a car or any of the trappings of respectability his father and his friends had enjoyed. That was before Soni sent him a brand new car on his thirty-fifth birthday.

He rued the fact that most of the things he had wished for all his life would not come easily to him. But Soni was the one to whom everything came easily: women, popularity, money and, it now seemed, an untimely end.

Abel arrived in Lagos on a Sunday afternoon lugging a tired old briefcase he had inherited from his father. It was an old Echolac with a combination lock. He had packed two pairs of jeans and three T-shirts as well as three boxer shorts and vests. He had his toothbrush, a hairbrush, a half-used bar of soap, Vaseline, toothpaste and an old towel. There was a pair of ageing black shoes that Soni had sent him for his wedding, wrapped in a black cellophane bag. He had also packed three books: the collected poems of T.S. Eliot, Christopher Okigbo's definitive collection of poems, *Labyrinths*, and the novel *A Mercy* by Toni Morrison.

Ada was at the park to pick him up. He saw her through the window before the bus came to a halt. She was as pretty as he remembered her, in a long, flowing white gown with floral designs on the chest.

She gave him a perfunctory hug as he stepped out of the bus and offered to take his briefcase.

'No thanks.'

'How was your trip?' she asked, leading the way to a black BMW X5.

Abel dumped his briefcase in the back and settled into the passenger seat. Up close, he could see that a child and the passing of time had had no effect on her. Ada still looked beautiful. More beautiful, it seemed, than she had been when he last saw her at the wedding in her lovely cream, off-the-shoulder wedding gown that showed off her flawless skin and ample bosom.

She was tall and dark, with those same pouty lips that Soni had admired. 'When I saw her that night,' he'd said, 'the first thing I noticed were her lips, and it was as if they were saying to me "kiss me, kiss me". So I walked up to her and said, "You have the best lips I have ever seen; would you let me kiss them?" She was with her friends and you know how girls can be. She just laughed and said in Igbo, "onye ala." I spoke back in Igbo, saying that yes she was right. Her beauty and perfect lips were driving me nuts. You trust your brother, we were kissing before we left that club and two weeks later she moved in with me.'

Abel could still see the twinkle in Soni's eyes as he told him how he and Ada met, that weekend when he came home to Asaba to inform him and their mother that he was getting married.

'What does she do?' Abel had asked. They were having drinks in Soni's suite at the Grand Hotel Asaba. With their father dead, Abel was the head of the family and Soni had come to inform him and ask for his blessing. But it was all a mere formality; Abel's opinion did not matter, though he was happy Soni was taking the trouble to seek his blessing. More so, considering the fact that they had fallen out after the unfortunate letter in which he'd railed against marrying a girl he met in the club.

'She just finished NYSC. She studied linguistics and, hold on, I know this one will interest you: she made a 2.1.' Soni smiled broadly.

'Anyone can get a 2.1,' Abel said, a tad bit too flippantly. He forced a nervous laugh. 'I don't mean it that way. You know I am always speaking out my thoughts.'

'No wahala, bros. I understand. You are my brother and I need you to be happy for me. Ada is a smart, pretty and sweet girl. Try and forget where I met her.'

Abel reached across the table and patted his brother's hand.

'I am happy for you, and if she makes you happy, then go for it.'

Three weeks later, a large parcel arrived from Lagos. Inside was an Italian-made, navy-blue, single-button suit, a spanking white shirt, a gold cravat, a Cesare Paciotti black leather belt, and a pair of black leather shoes by the same designer. There was even a pair of black socks and a white handkerchief with one hundred thousand naira, cash, which Soni had sent to enable Abel to fly to Lagos. Soni did not want his best man to miss the wedding under any pretext.

'How is your son?' Abel asked Ada as they made the turn from Adekunle onto Third Mainland Bridge.

'Fine. His name is Zeal.'

'Zeal. Soni gave his son an English name?' Soni had rebelled against his name, Sunderland, changing it to Soni the moment he could.

'Zeal is not an English name. It is short for Zealinjo. Flee from evil.'

'Oh, sorry about that,' Abel said recalling at that moment that Soni had actually sent him a text with all the names and had even asked him to propose one. 'Do you think he knows what is going on? The fact that his father is missing?'

'Not really. You know your brother used to travel a lot. But I'm sure he can feel that this trip is different. I don't think Zeal is too young to realise that this trip has lasted a bit too long.'

'Thank God for innocence,' Abel said. 'What are the police saying?'

'They say they are investigating.' Abel thought she heard her voice break. 'I haven't given them any money in the past few days and I think they are slacking.'

'What did they do when they were not slacking?' he asked, without meaning to. 'Don't mind me. I tend to voice my thoughts.'

'You also tend to write them out,' she said, looking at him.

'Ada, you look more beautiful when you are angry.' He laughed and tried to change the topic, but she kept staring at him with a face that mirrored her rage. 'We have had this conversation before,' he said finally.

'Yes, and we were interrupted when Soni walked in. You think every girl you meet in a club is a prostitute?'

'I never said that.'

'But you implied it. My parents are both lecturers, like you. PhD holders. My two siblings are medical doctors. You don't know me,' she said with feeling.

'I agree and I am sorry. That letter was meant for my brother.' His eyes went from her face to the road. It was a Sunday afternoon and traffic was light. Still, he didn't want her taking her eyes off the road for too long.

She sighed as she turned off the bridge. They drove in silence for the rest of the trip from Dolphin Estate into Osborne, past Kingsway Road, on to Falomo, down to Ozumba Mbadiwe and the new toll plaza, all the way to the magnificent mansion Soni had erected just off Admiralty Way in Lekki Phase 1.

'You should stay in his room. My nanny is in your room.'

'My room?'

'Yes, your room. Soni made it especially for you but I brought her up when your brother went missing. I needed company here in the family wing,' she said pushing a door open.

The room was large and done up in white and black. It had a masculine feel; a man cave. Abel could see Soni in every detail, right down to the cursive above the headboard: 9 inches is here!

The marauding dick had finally found a home.

'You are sure you are OK with this?' Abel asked turning to look at her.

'Well, there is a connecting door to my room. I am OK so long as you keep it locked. If you keep the key in the lock, I can't open it from my end. So it's OK.'

'Thank you.' He sat on the bed.

'You are welcome. His clothes are in the closet. You guys wear the same size. You may need them because you will be meeting important people.'

'And my clothes won't be good enough,' Abel said before he realised what he was saying.

'I don't mean it that way, but Soni is always giving away his clothes. I would prefer they went to family.'

'I'm family?' Abel began before he caught himself mid-sentence. 'Cool.'

She opened her mouth as if to speak, thought better of it, and made for the door. But then she stopped mid-stride, her hand on the doorknob, and began to speak, her back turned to him.

'We need money to eat and pay drivers, house helps and other domestic staff, as well as staff in the office. They haven't been paid for the last month. I will call Santos. He will take you around. He used to follow Soni around. He knows everyone and has been helping draw up names and leads for the police. He will come in tomorrow morning. I will give you all the cheque books and account numbers. But first you have to see the lawyer to help you sort out issues at the probate registry.'

'OK.' Abel suddenly felt overwhelmed by it all. Two days earlier he was just a lecturer eking out a precarious existence in a hovel in Asaba. Now he was in a mansion in Lagos, wondering what had shifted in the foundation of things.

'Bring Zeal,' he said. 'Let me play with my son.'

'My son,' she said and walked out.

WAIT AND SEE

Santos came early the next morning. He used to ride around shotgun with Soni because, as Abel got to learn, his brother never trusted anyone enough to drive him. That was why, on the day he disappeared, they found his car in a ditch in Shomolu, the engine running, the speakers blaring Fela.

Abel remembered Santos as Ikechukwu, a snotty-nosed kid who loved biscuits and used to spend his holidays with them. He was a cousin of sorts who had lost his mother at an early age and ended up being passed around a cast of uncles and aunts. They called him Ten Biscuits because once, while on holiday at their house, he had gone begging for biscuits from a neighbour who ran a small supermarket. Two silly boys who lived down the road had told Ikechukwu that they would give him ten biscuits if he allowed them to smear a hot Chinese balm on his eyes. Ikechukwu agreed. His screams had alerted the neighbours, who rushed out to administer first aid.

After his eyes had been washed clean and he could identify the boys, they discovered that Ikechukwu had been clutching the sodden biscuits in his palm, all the while.

'Ten Biscuits!' Abel yelled as Santos sauntered into the living room where he was watching CNN.

'Bros, easy o,' he whispered in Abel's ear as they hugged. 'My name is now Santos o.'

'Santos, Santos,' he said as their embrace broke.

'Welcome, bros. You have been suffering in Asaba when your brother is a king in Lagos,' he said in Igbo.

'I have come to my brother's kingdom,' Abel countered, and they both laughed.

'Welcome bros. Where are you going today? Iyawo say we get many places to go today,' Santos said, switching to pidgin.

Abel told him he needed to go to the lawyer, then to the bank to see whether he could free up the account and get some money. That was paramount.

'No yawa,' Santos said. 'Bros Sabato has plenty accounts but I will take you to the banks where there is plenty money.'

Sorting out the legal issues took days and by the sixth, Abel was tired and broke and frustrated. According to the bank, Soni was missing, not dead, so it was difficult to invoke the power of next of kin.

So, back and forth to the lawyers Abel went. An affidavit was sworn, documents were provided, letters were written, but at the end of the day it was Santos who came up with a bit of peculiar Lagos wisdom that helped them make headway.

'Bros, I no sure say this your court matter go work o,' Santos told him as they left the lawyer's office that morning. 'Sabato is still missing so e go hard. Let's go to one of the bank managers I know and offer him something. He will let us have some money to run things until we sort out the court wahala.'

The bank manager was a smallish, fair-skinned man in a well-cut suit. His fingers were manicured and coated with transparent nail polish. His shoes gleamed and he had the air of someone who liked to look good; the kind of person who bought his clothes based on what models were wearing in the glossy spreads of *GQ* or *Vogue*.

But the moment he spoke, Abel saw it all fall away. He had a thick accent that Abel immediately placed as Bendel, the old name for what used to be Delta and Edo states. It was the thick residual accent of a boy who grew up in the village before fate thrust him into Lagos.

As he spoke Abel looked at his hands again, at the fingers he kept clasping and unclasping. They were peasant's fingers masked with a patina of gentility. They were the hands of a man who had grown up on a farm and who, having escaped, would do everything to never go back.

Abel knew people like him. He met them first at the university. They would arrive as bush and timid as they came, but by the second semester they would be affecting an annoying American accent. Their voices, with the fake accent and half-realised drawl, always reminded him of someone with body odour, the kind that remains long after the person has left the room.

'So, you want some money and you don't wanna wait for the legal processes to be completed, is that what you are saying?' he asked, his beady eyes flipping from Abel to Santos.

'Basically, yes,' Abel answered.

'That's not legal, you know. We could all get into trouble.'

'Bros, na help we need,' Santos butted in, all solicitous and Lagos-like. It was something Abel would come to recognise: a tone of voice and posture that said, dude, I know I am begging but you can't say no.

'Help us and my bros here go also make sure say something drop. We know say Sabato has a huge sum in your bank. The last statement you sent showed say he has one hundred and thirty-two million naira here, abi?'

The bank manager smiled as if impressed. Abel was impressed that Santos had that figure.

'So, imagine say you give us ten million. My bros here go drop one point five million for you; that's a cool 15 per cent. So, anytime we need money, we will show and it's the same arrangement all over,' Santos told him, switching fluidly from pidgin to English.

'Una no fit make am 25 per cent?' the bank manager asked, all pretences at Americanese gone. His small eyes shone with greed. 'I gotta sort out other people,' he added when he caught the look on Abel's face.

'Bros, Sabato get plenty money for different banks. If you don't accept our 15 per cent we will go to another bank,' Santos told him without frills, his gaze level with the bank manager's.

Silence stretched the moment for a few seconds before the bank manager cracked a smile and stretched out his hand.

'Kai, dis bros you harsh,' he said regressing to his origins. 'Give me a few days to sort this out. I will give you a call once it's ready. You have a card?'

Abel shook his head and wrote down his phone number on a bright pink sticky-note pad on the manager's table.

'Thanks guys,' the bank manager said as he opened the door to his office. 'I will give you a call.'

In the car Abel turned to look at Santos.

'Bros, corruption is another name for Lagos,' Santos said before Abel could find the words he was looking for. 'Nobody come Lagos to count bridge. You help me, I help you — everyone happy. The guy is taking serious risk and we are paying for the risk. But look am well; we get money to run things, e get something for him wahala. Everybody is happy.'

'If I had gone alone, I would never have known how to do that,' Abel said, still amazed at how easily Santos had pushed forward with the proposal.

'No shame for Lagos, o. If you shame hunger go kill you, bros. That's one thing I learn from Bros Sabato and that manager: no dey play with him cut. Na deal man be dat.'

'You knew him before now?' Abel asked.

'Yes o. Sabato is a special customer and he told me this funny gist about the manager.' Santos switched from pidgin to Igbo like a crazy driver veering from lane to lane.

The story was about Soni and an old friend, someone with whom he had done a job. When the money was paid, it was routed through the same bank manager, although he was just the head of operations at a small branch at the time. It wasn't much — a mere three million naira — but it was a lot back then because Soni and his friend were just starting out.

The manager had packed the cash into two Ghana-must-go bags, and spread out on the table was three hundred thousand naira, which he believed was his cut – a cool 10 per cent.

But there was trouble brewing: getting greedy, Soni's friend had called ahead and persuaded the bank manager not to split the remaining two million seven hundred thousand equally. So, when they arrived, Soni's bag had one million two hundred, while the other guy's had one million five hundred thousand naira.

'Bros, you should have seen the fight,' Santos said, getting into the story as if he had been there. 'Sabato didn't waste any time in attacking his friend. There was blood everywhere by the time mobile policemen came in to break them up. It was the mobile policemen who saved the day. They almost sacked the guy but Sabato said he was happy how the guy quickly shared out the money equally and asked them to leave. So, when money came bros made sure he remained loyal to the bank manager. That's why I said we should come and see him. I know he likes money and he and Sabato go back a long way

—

Soni's office was in Apapa, off Creek Road and close to the wharf. He had a staff of about twelve. Abel addressed them later that morning in the tastefully furnished conference room. Though he was a lecturer and quite used to speaking, it felt strange sitting there with men and women seated around the table, some as old as his parents, hanging on to his every word.

It felt surreal as he signed cheques running into millions to cover admin costs and pay salaries for all staff members when his own salary was nothing to write home about. It all needed getting used to but there was no time to adjust. He was diving headlong into things.

Back at home, he was surprised to find that they needed close to a quarter of a million naira to keep the house running.

'Soni gives me two hundred thousand as a monthly housekeeping allowance,' Ada told him when he expressed shock. Abel was too ashamed to tell her that that was close to his salary for three months.

It was a strange feeling having all that money and being in control of it. Stranger still was being able to spend hundreds of thousands in one day and not wake up in the middle of the night terrified that you had done something stupid to imperil yourself.

With money, he could also rev up the search for his missing brother and take it farther than Ada had. After all, that was the main reason why he was in Lagos.

'I know somebody for Area C,' Santos told him one morning.

'But the case na for Panti,' Abel told him.

'I know bros, but police is police and it's the same language they all speak.'

A stranger in Lagos, Abel was beginning to relax about letting Santos steer him around, even though he had a niggling feeling that Santos wasn't doing it just to be helpful. Abel sensed that there was something else at play, but he pushed the thought aside, putting it down to the fact that Lagos was beginning to make him paranoid.

The Area C police station was a charred ruin. At the entrance to the station, two burnt motorcycles sat like gargoyles in front of a medieval cathedral while burnt vehicles littered the station grounds like fallen soldiers. Inside, Abel and Santos met two bored-looking policemen; a fat one and a thin one.

Abel was actually surprised to find a thin policeman who was not a rookie. He always thought of Nigerian policemen as corpulent and shifty-eyed men in dirty uniforms trying to ensnare you.

The fat one was dressed in a white buba and sokoto and kept nodding off as they made enquiries. Santos couldn't find the phone number of the officer they had come to see so they decided to wait for him.

'Inspector Agboola will soon come in. I think he is IPO on a case that went to court today. I have sent him a text,' the fat guy told them and immediately nodded off.

Abel sat on the tall stool they had been offered as Santos told him the story of how the station came to be the charred ruin it was. It had been razed by soldiers following an altercation with policemen who had arrested and detained a soldier for a minor traffic offence. The angry soldiers had taken the station hostage, freed their colleague and torched the building.

'This place was like a war zone that day. Soldiers, their head is not correct o.'

A woman selling gala and coke passed by and Abel, who had left home without breakfast, waved her over. Santos declined. Abel ordered for himself and the two policemen. He stared, amazed, at how the fat guy could chew and snore at the same time.

'Why do you want to see Inspector Agboola,' the thin guy asked with his mouth full. The drink and sausage rolls had made him amiable.

'My brother is missing. They found his car in a ditch with music on, but he was gone. It's almost a month now.'

'What kind of car was he driving?'

'A Jaguar.'

'That's not a small car. What does he do for a living?'

'Business,' Santos piped up. He didn't want Abel providing the wrong answer.

'Business, eh?' the policeman said, looking at Santos. 'Well, that's what usually happens to businessmen in this Lagos. That's what happens to Lagos Big Boys.'

He raised his Coke to his lips, took a long sip, swished it around his mouth and swallowed loudly.

'This kind of case can be difficult to solve,' he continued. 'If he had gone missing after boarding a commercial bus, we would say One Chance or kidnappers or we can attribute it to some talismanic occurrence. But when a man goes missing from his luxury car, hmmm, water don pass garri.'

'He must be dead,' the fat policeman said and Abel jumped, startled by his deep voice. 'Or has there been a ransom demand?'

'No,' Abel said. 'No demands.'

'No demands, hmmm. That means that it is not a kidnap and if it is not a kidnap that means that the people who took him knew why they took him; to take him out of the picture. Abi, your brother and madam dey get problems? You think the man has run away from his troublesome wife?'

'No. They don't have issues like that,' Santos said.

'Like how then?' the thin guy asked.

'They usually have normal husband and wife issues, that's all,' Santos offered quickly. 'My bros like babes and babes can cause trouble at home.' With policemen, you didn't give open-ended answers; they were always pouncing on what one left unsaid.

'If you drive a Jaguar, babes won't be your problem,' the fat guy said. Abel was impressed. Even though he had been nodding off he had managed to soak everything in. 'Anyway, if you ask me I will say it will be a miracle for your brother to be found. Businessmen pile up two things in this Lagos: money and enemies. This looks like his enemies got him. But don't take my word for it. Let's wait and see what Panti people come up with.' He stopped to pick up his ringing phone. 'Inspector, OK, OK. I will tell them. No wahala.'

The inspector had been held up so he had called to ask for Santos' number. They exchanged details and then Abel and Santos headed to the car. As Santos pulled out of the station, he turned to Abel.

'Bros, no vex o but I want to tell you something.'

'Sure. What?'

'Nothing much bros, it is just that you have become Lagos Big Boy now so it's not pure for you to be chopping gala like that for street.'

Abel looked at Santos, with his afro, neatly ironed polo shirt, well-fitted jeans and bright red canvas shoes, and smiled. He was beginning to feel something for this crazy, peculiar city called Lagos.

'I hear you Santos. I hear you,' Abel said tapping him on the shoulder.

THE BEAST WITH BARED FANGS

Lagos is a beast with bared fangs and a voracious appetite for human flesh. Walk through its neighbourhoods, from the gated communities of Ikoyi and Victoria Island to Lekki and beyond, to the riotous warrens of streets and alleyways on the mainland, and you can tell that this is a carnivorous city. Life is not just brutish – it is short.

In Lagos, one is sometimes struck by the scary fact that some crazed evil genius may have invented a million quick, sad ways for people to die: fall off a molue, fall prey to ritual killers, be pushed out of a moving danfo by one-chance robbers, fall into an open gutter in the rain, be electrocuted in your shop, be killed by your domestic staff, jump off the Third Mainland Bridge, get shot by armed robbers, get hit by a stray bullet from a policeman extorting motorists, get rammed by a vehicle that veers off the road into the pedestrian's walkway, die in a fire, get crushed in a collapsing building. You could count the ways and there would still be many others.

Yet, like crazed moths disdaining the rage of the flame, we keep gravitating towards Lagos, compelled by some centrifugal force that defies reason and willpower. We come, take our chances, hoping that we will be luckier than the next man, willing ourselves to believe that while our fortune lies here, the myriad evils that traverse the streets of Lagos will never meet us with bared fangs.

Abel and Santos were in Mushin when Lagos bared its fangs. There are no quiet streets in Mushin. It crackles with electric intensity and ripples with animosity. It is as if everyone, from shifty-eyed men to paranoid women, feels you are out to get them.

Mushin is a tough land with serious turf wars. Rivals from different gangs and factions – especially of the National Union of Road Transport Workers – prowl the streets at midday with pump-action guns, wild looks and well-smoked joints stuck between fat, black lips.

Loud music blares out of speakers; boisterous, energetic music from the likes of Pasuma, Saheed Osupa, Wande Coal and even zanga master Durella. These are young men who once prowled these streets, who got their start in life here before success ferried them out to safer locales. Now, the young men and women left behind play their music as talismans of hope that one day the ships of their destiny will berth at a good port and their luck would also turn.

Abel came with Santos, who now passed for his PA and driver. Santos had chosen for them to go in a Toyota Camry.

'Mushin no be better place,' he told Abel in the morning. 'Make we no carry big motor.'

They had come to meet a man whom Santos called Bros but whose name, Abel learnt, was Raimi. To Santos, everyone was Bros.

Raimi worked at the post office in Onipanu. He'd had a run-in with Soni in the early days, but they'd made their peace and become friends. He helped Soni with his waybills while Soni, in appreciation and his usual large-hearted way, had settled him well: built him a small house on the land he inherited from his father and gained his trust.

But in Lagos, especially in a place like Mushin, trust is a shape-shifter, a mercurial being with ever-shifting allegiances. Trust is not a boulder one leans on with confidence. It is quicksand at best: neither terra nor wholly firma.

It was a few minutes past noon on a Saturday, but you wouldn't have known it from the bottles of beer scattered all over the table set outside a small bar. It seemed as if they had been drinking and partying from the night before.

'That your brother na bad spirit,' Raimi said as they shook hands. Two of his friends made way for them to sit. From the way he called Soni a bad spirit, Abel could tell it was a compliment.

'Mama Risi, bring drinks for my friends,' Raimi said to the owner of the shop. 'Na my better friends be dis. Bring peppered chicken too.'

'Wetin bros go drink?' a wisp of a girl asked, wiping her wet hands on her dirty apron.

They placed their orders and Abel smiled his thanks to Raimi.

'Dat your brother na better person,' Raimi said, shushing Abel's thanks with a wave of his hand as he started to roll a big fat joint. 'If I am a woman, he will fuck me till I die.' Abel smiled and nodded. This, he knew, was another compliment.

'Soni has been missing now for twenty-nine days. Nobody don see am since,' Abel told him, sure that he already knew.

'I hear and e pain me,' Raimi said, reaching for his matchbox. 'Wetin police dem dey talk?' He struck a match to light his joint, pulled on it and extended it to Abel. Abel shook his head.

'Santos, dis your egbon na gentleman o. I surprise say e dey even drink stout sef.' Raimi laughed. The laughter grew into a cough that rattled on for a while.

'E dey drink stout,' Santos said, puffing on the joint that had just been passed to him and ignoring Abel's look of disapproval.

'E resemble Sabato for face but ah,' Raimi said, rising and pounding his fist against his chest like King Kong. 'Nobody fit be like Sabato Rabato. Sabato Rabato na ogbologbo. Nowhere we e no fit enter, nothing wey e no fit drink, no woman wey e no fit chop. Ah, Sabato Rabato, e no go better for dem.'

His friends chorused, 'Ase!' and snapped their fingers above their heads to ward off evil.

'So, wetin you say you wan show me?' Raimi asked, all business now as he settled back in his seat.

'I hear say you and Soni were supposed to meet the day he disappeared. E tell Santos say e dey come see you,' Abel said, see-sawing between English and pidgin.

He had rehearsed this opening for days, trying to find the right words to express his intentions and concerns without giving offence or making Raimi feel that they were accusing him. They were on his turf and it wouldn't do to antagonise him in his own backyard.

Raimi didn't answer. He took a long drag and held the smoke, eyes bulging. When he spoke, smoke escaped from his nose and ears.

'My broda, I get small house for yonder,' he said eventually, pointing behind Abel. 'Two rooms. Na my own. I am a landlord for this Mushin. I don't pay rent to any gaddem landlord. My house get DSTV. E get borehole. Last year, when I celebrate fifty years, Sabato dash me tokunbo motor, drop-top Golf GTI. Na the money wey e dey dash me na im I take build dat house. Why you think say I go spoil something wey dey pay my life, eh?' Abel opened his mouth to say he was not accusing him, but Raimi signalled for him to be quiet.

'I no follow you vex. Woman looking for her missing pikin does not have time to say "excuse me, sah, excuse me, sah". No be so?' His friends nodded. 'Sabato get appointment with me dat Saturday. E suppose bring one waybill come. I wait for am, e no show. I call Santos, Santos say Sabato send am go see one olopa for Agege police station, abi?' Santos nodded in agreement. 'So, na only Sabato comot from house. E no reach our post office and e no come here.'

'I see one waybill inside one envelope for Soni room,' Abel said. 'Sabato write your name on the envelope. Santos, please get it from the briefcase.'

As Santos rose, a group of five people walked into view. They had formed a ring around a young man. His young but wizened face was a collage of emotions: fear, defiance and something old and mean. He was sweating and saying 'Na my money I come for. After person do freedom, oga suppose settle am.'

'Oga say make you come back next week,' a voice told him.

'Every time, come back next week, come back next week. One year don pass now. Na my money I want.'

Abel was not paying attention. He was looking across at Santos and also trying to pay attention to whatever it was Raimi was saying, but Raimi was mixing his words with Yoruba and Abel was lost.

He sipped his drink and looked up again to see what Santos, who had the boot open, was doing.

The argument was raging now. Voices were raised, threats were whistling above their heads. They were speaking rapid-fire pidgin and Yoruba.

Abel was suddenly distracted by Santos, who ran back to whisper that he couldn't open the Echolac briefcase and didn't want to bring it out because of the money inside.

'Excuse me,' Abel said to Raimi, and walked back to the car, leaving Santos at the table. He popped open the boot and was typing in the combination when he heard a slap and sharp cry.

'You. Iwo. You think you have strong head, abi.' A new man had appeared and slapped the boy who had been demanding his money. He must be the master, the Oga the boy has come to see, Abel thought. He watched him kick at the boy, who staggered back into a fence. Cornered, he reached for a long metal pole and brandished it like a spear. The crowd jumped back each time he swung it. His former master's face glistened with sweat, his pot belly heaving and shiny from perspiration. His crowd gathered behind him, booing the boy but jumping back out of harm's way.

'Oho, you don grow now, abi?' The master lunged at the boy, who ducked and swung the pole in a fine arc. Then there was silence.

The master stood there with a surprised look on his face, his mouth half open, his hand on his stomach. Then Abel saw the red seeping through his fingers. The pole had sliced his belly open. As he staggered back, his intestines escaped his fingers and spilled out of his gut.

'Santos! Santos!' Abel heard himself scream as he slammed the boot shut and got into the car.

His scream seemed to have broken the spell and set everyone free from some cosmic grip. The boy tried to run but was tackled to the ground. He screamed as someone stabbed him with the pole, then staggered up and began to run, the pole impaled in his side, blood trailing behind him.

The street was alive. Men and boys were exiting houses armed with dangerous things. Santos dodged a blow as he crossed the street to the car. Abel's hands were shaking badly but he finally managed to get the key in the ignition and turn on the engine. He engaged a gear and drove off, yelling at Santos to jump in. A rod smashed into their windscreen, which exploded, showering him with shards of glass like hailstones.

Abel stepped on the gas pedal and knocked two guys off the road as he tried to see through the shattered glass. Santos was half inside the car, his legs sticking out of the window. He screamed as someone slashed him with a dagger. Abel turned to look – a bad move. When he turned back to the road, they were heading straight for a car that seemed to have appeared out of nowhere.

They collided at 60 miles per hour. Santos was screaming and men were approaching. Abel was stunned by the crash but his adrenaline was pumping. He shook the blur away and looked around. They were in a dead end.

'Bros, make we run,' Santos said, scrambling out of the car. He yanked Abel's door open, pulled him out and then they ran. When Abel looked back, three guys were in hot pursuit.

They scaled the fence behind a house and headed into another street. The commotion had reached there too and there was rage in the air.

Abel looked back. The three were still chasing them. One had a limp. He was one of the guys he had knocked out of their path, which explained why they were giving chase.

'Bros, oya turn, enter here,' Santos said pulling Abel into a corner.

A young woman was spreading clothes on a line and was surprised to see them.

'Santos, what are you looking for in the afternoon? My mother is at home o,' she said with a shy smile.

'Hide us, abeg, hide us,' Santos said. She opened the door to their house in one swift move and pushed them in.

Abel did not leave Soni's house for two weeks, until the money he left with Ada ran out and he was compelled to go to the bank. Santos reported to the house every day, but Abel just ignored him and the itinerary he presented. Losing the Toyota Camry, his Echolac briefcase, the documents inside, the cash – all six hundred thousand of it – and escaping death by the whiskers had left him petrified.

They hadn't left Mushin until late at night and when they did it was in the back of a pickup truck that smelled badly of stale beer. Celina, the girl who had given them cover, had arranged for a cousin to help them leave. They had hidden at the back of his rickety pickup under a tattered tarpaulin.

Now, too scared to venture out, Abel sat at home and watched CNN.

'Sonny has paid for a DSTV subscription for five years so we don't have any problems with cable TV,' Ada told him.

He couldn't afford cable TV in Asaba, but after two weeks he knew all the programmes as well as the anchors and correspondents. He liked Isha Sesay the best. He was always surprised by her baby face. Abel loved listening to her.

When he was not watching CNN, he played with his nephew, whom he was beginning to feel thought Abel was his daddy. They played with his toys and Abel read to him from the over one hundred books Soni had left him.

'How come Soni bought him all these books?' Abel asked Ada one evening after reading to Zeal. 'He didn't even like to read.'

Ada didn't speak for a while. She regarded her brother-in-law for a moment, then said, 'You know, Soni thought you were the best thing since sliced bread.' Her beautiful lips curled up into a smile as she watched Abel's shocked expression. 'He always wondered what you would think or say. He said you were well read and knew everything about everything. He worshipped you.'

'Really?' Abel blurted out the word before he could stop himself.

'Really,' she said, and walked away.

When Abel finally summoned up courage to leave the house, he decided he would not go beyond the island and the bank. He had, at the back of his mind, the irrational fear that he could run into one of the boys from Mushin on the mainland.

Their first trip was to Ikoyi to visit a woman he had spoken to on the phone and whom Santos introduced first as Soni's customer then later as Soni's lover.

'You say Soni was sleeping with her?'

'Yes, o. She is a widow. Her husband die for that Ejigbo plane crash and na bros dey service am since.'

In 1992, a military C-130H aircraft conveying an elite class of military officers had gone down in the swamps of Ejigbo. Many suspected that the plane had been rigged by the then military president, who was afraid of being overthrown. The crash decimated an entire corps of future military leaders.

'How come you know that?' Abel asked.

'Haba, bros,' Santos said. 'I am not a small boy. Bros no dey let me enter with am and when he come out he will be smelling like someone who has done something.'

'Done what thing?' Abel asked and Santos laughed.

'Bros, you are not a small boy, haba! What does a man and woman do inside the room, ah ah, you should know? The way Iyawo is looking at you sef, it looks like she is liking you small-small.'

'Santos, keep driving.'

The house was a lovely mansion in Parkview Estate, Ikoyi where, Santos told Abel, a plot of land sold for about $2 million, even though the roads were potholed and filled with water.

The woman welcomed them in a flowing gown reminiscent of Stevie Nicks of Fleetwood Mac. Abel could see that she wasn't wearing any panties as she stood silhouetted in the doorway, waving them in.

'You are Abel, abi?' she asked as she settled at the head of an expansive dining table with twelve chairs.

'Yes,' Abel replied, intimidated by the grandeur. Though not nearly as grand as Soni's, the woman's house still spoke of affluence and wealth.

'Your brother thought you were the salt of the earth. Are you ten inches?

Abel shook his head. 'I have never measured it,' he said with a smile.

'You don't have to. It doesn't help anyone. I told Soni he was nothing without his dick. I made a big mistake. I told my friends about him, nine inches and all. They rushed after him and he thought he had arrived. They were all married. I was the widow. I honoured my husband for seven years before I met Soni. He was smart, funny, good-looking, fun to have around and very ambitious.' She suddenly turned to look at Santos. 'Hey, who is this smiling monkey?'

'My cousin,' Abel said.

'Tell him to wait outside,' the woman said, as if Santos was not there. Abel waved at Santos to leave.

'Are you married?' she asked. Abel shook his head. 'Are you fucking his wife?'

'Of course not!' Abel shouted and she laughed.

'She is a lovely girl, so did you mean of course not or not yet?' Abel had no answer. 'Let's eat,' she said, and they did.

The meal was excellent. Quail and salmon, snail and gizzard with jollof and Chinese rice, all washed down with red wine.

'Come to the garden,' she said pushing back her chair and leading the way.

The garden was a part of the house. It had real grass on the floor, flowers on the side, and a transparent roof that gave it a cool greenhouse effect.

'If it gets too hot, we retract the roof,' she told him, following his gaze. 'Do you smoke?' She pulled a pack of cigarettes from her handbag.

Abel shook his head.

She lit the slim cigarette, inhaled deeply and held the smoke.

'I have two kids. They were in senior secondary when my husband died. I saw them through the university and finished this house before I looked at any man and it wasn't even a man that I found but a boy – your brother.'

'How did you meet my brother?'

'He came to me. I was at a boutique. I tried on these sandals, thought they were too expensive and put them back. I was getting into my car when he walked up to me and handed me a bag with the shoes inside.'

'The slippers?' Abel corrected her.

'Yes, the slippers. Your brother was a real charmer. I asked him, "Did you guys change your mind?" assuming his boss had sent him to give me the slippers at the price I had bargained. But he shook his head and said, "I don't work there."

"So, what's this about?" I asked getting a bit apprehensive. He said, "I saw you try them on. I thought it would be a real shame if you didn't have them. My name is Sabato."

'He had lovely manicured fingers. I was forty-six. I had not had sex for seven years but when I touched that twenty-six year old boy, I felt my body come alive. We were lovers by that evening.' She took a long drag. 'Let's have some cognac, do you mind?'

Abel did not. She pressed a bell and a domestic help appeared.

'Get the Courvoisier,' she told him, crossing her long legs. 'So, I asked you before about his wife. What's going on there?'

'Nothing. We don't agree.'

'Why? Did you try something funny?'

'No. Old history; something that happened before they got married.'

'I remember. Something about the nightclub, right?' Abel nodded. 'She will forgive. Women are forgiving. That's why God gave us the ability to have babies.'

Abel thought about that as his drink was poured but couldn't see how it was related to anything, so he asked a question.

'Did Soni confide a lot in you?'

'Yes, he did. I was like a mother to him and he was an open book, easy to read. He had a stubborn streak though.'

And he was fucking his mother, Abel thought, then smothered it.

'So, did he tell you about what he was working on? Something you think could have led to his disappearance?'

The lady stood up and began to pace with her glass in one hand and a freshly lit cigarette in the other.

'Soni was bound to die like this,' she said stopping in front of Abel.

'Die? He is missing.' Abel said, sitting up.

'Missing? Accept it, Abel. Soni will never be found, not alive. This is Lagos. Some people have to die. Their blood is sacrifice to the hungry beast that is Lagos. That is how it is.'

'So, you think he is dead?'

'I don't think; I know he is dead, Abel, and if you are truly his brother you must feel it too.' She settled in the seat beside him and took Abel's hand. 'Do you know the things your brother was into? Bad things, criminal activities. Do you know the kind of men whose wives he was sleeping with? Your brother had many enemies. Too many people had reasons to wish him dead.'

'Did you wish him dead?' Abel asked, taking his hand from hers and looking straight into her eyes.

'I needed him too much to wish him dead. He was good in bed, although sometimes a big dick is not enough.' She rose and drained her drink.

Abel stood too.

'I lost a husband in a plane crash and I know what it means not to have a body to bury. But we choose our paths in life. Your brother chose his.'

THE AXE HEAD

Abel could hear a woman yelling as he awoke.

It was a Saturday and he had hoped to lie in until noon, at least. The whole process of searching and meeting with various characters was beginning to take its toll and all he wanted to do was laze in bed.

By the time he made it to the restroom and back he could hear Ada pacifying the loud woman.

'Auntie no vex o. I am really sorry,' Ada was saying.

'Sorry ke; that's all you will say? My brother is missing and all you can tell me is sorry. I had to hear it from strangers. And Chiedu has been in Lagos since and he didn't even bother to come and see me, eh? Where is he? Where is Chiedu?'

She was referring to Abel.

He pulled on a pair of jeans and threw on a T-shirt, wondering who could be causing all that commotion.

When he stepped out, a chubby-faced woman was standing in the upstairs living room and Ada was on her knees, begging her to sit down. It took a moment for Abel to register, then he cried out, 'Auntie Ekwi!'

Her hug was full and encompassing, crushing Abel against her ample bosom. She had always been well endowed and Abel remembered how, as teenagers, he and Soni, with Soni in the lead, would stand behind the bathroom and watch her bathe, fascinated by the huge breasts resting on her slight frame. Now, the years and child bearing had balanced things out.

'Chiedu, you came into Lagos and you didn't come to see me or ask after me,' she said to him in Igbo.

'Auntie no vex,' Abel told her in pidgin before switching to Igbo. 'Auntie, the things my eyes have seen, eh.' He steered her to a couch. They sat down and Ada took the seat next to them.

'What did your eye see that made you unable to call and say, "Ekwi, I am in town o." Haba, I had to hear about my own brother from a stranger, a complete stranger and at the salon for that matter. What happened to Sabato?'

Abel was surprised at how, even though his aunt had called him 'Chiedu', the name everyone called him by as a child, she, like everyone else called Soni by his *nom de guerre*, Sabato. It was a clear sign of his full transformation; he had descended into the underworld of Lagos and jettisoned his old life. While Abel remained Abel Chiedu Dike, his younger brother had been rechristened. He would forever remain Sabato Rabato.

'Auntie, it's a long story. They found his car in Shomolu, half inside the gutter. The engine was on and the music too, but Soni was gone. I received a text and I came down as fast as I could. We have visited the police and many of the people he used to deal with. No one seems to know anything. So we keep searching.'

'Does Sister know?' she asked, referring to Abel's mum, who was in the village and hadn't been informed.

'No. Ah, we can't tell her something like that.'

Soni was their mother's favourite and news of him missing would devastate her. However, he also knew that, because the whole family had a sense of the kind of business he indulged in, the one that had made him an insanely rich man, they had always half expected this kind of news. It was simple: as with the spouse of a man who has gone to war, there is always a sense of dread when there is a knock at the door. That was what it was really like for many people living in Lagos, especially those like Soni, who dealt in the kind of things he dealt with. Soni was a true soldier and Lagos was his battlefield. It was not difficult to see why he could so easily become a statistic.

'You know this is not something you leave to policemen alone. They will take your money and do nothing and if your mother is not aware I cannot sit down and do nothing. What kind of aunt would I be if I heard and did nothing, eh?'

Abel knew the question wasn't meant to be answered so he just made the right noises.

'I know a man; he prays and he sees things. We have to go and see him for prayers. He can help us where the police can't. We have to go and see him.'

Abel knew she wasn't asking for their permission. She was giving an order. As his mother's youngest sister, she was like a mini-mother.

Ada made breakfast, and after they'd eaten they all they piled into her BMW. Auntie Ekwi directed them to a place in Shomolu, off Morocco.

Once clear of the Island, Ada turned off Third Mainland Bridge into Adekunle, then drove the length of Herbert Macaulay and past Sabo bus stop until they got to Jibowu where she then turned into the road that led to Yaba College of Technology.

They drove left, past the building that used to serve as headquarters for highlife maestro Oliver De Coque's booking office, then right and straight past the gate that led to the military barracks in Yaba.

The road ahead split into three; one that led to Jibowu, which was where they had come from, one that went straight to Bajulaiye and the heart of Shomolu. Auntie Ekwi asked Ada to make a left and they drove into the third one, Morocco Street, past the Morocco family residence, which now had a telecom mast sticking out above the fence like a rude phallus. They drove as if they were heading to Onipanu then made a quick turn. There were two more turns before Auntie Ekwi told them they were there.

'Iyawo,' she said to Ada, using a Yoruba term that signified 'our wife'. 'Oya, clear well from the road, so no one will *brush* your car.'

Ada parked and Auntie Ekwi directed them into a bustling compound with a dim corridor and as they walked down to the back where the prayer house was, Abel wondered why the corridors that ran through the middle of tenement houses were always dark.

The prophet was dressed in a flowing white gown and had a red sash tied around his waist.

'Welcome, my children,' he said even though he didn't look much older than Abel.

He produced a bowl of water and asked them to wash their hands.

'He that seeks must come with clean hands and a pure heart,' he intoned. 'Wash your hands and confess your sins that our prayers may not be hindered.'

They washed and waited.

He took up the bowl, raised it above each person's head, muttered something and then went outside and poured it into the gutter that ran by the side of the church.

'My Lord, I called yesterday and you asked us to come today,' Auntie Ekwi began. 'We need your help. The police are trying but our brother is still missing. His wife is here and his son is at home. This is his brother. We want answers. Help us to go to God in prayer and we shall be grateful.'

If he had heard Auntie Ekwi, the prophet showed no sign of it. His eyes were squeezed shut and a vein stood out magnificently on his temple. He seemed to be concentrating intensely.

'The man of God asked, "Where did it fall?"' the prophet began, circling the room with slow steps, his eyes shut tight.

'And what happened next? "When he showed him the place, Elisha cut a stick and threw it there, and made the iron float." What we seek Lord Jehovah, send it up to us. Give us light where all is darkness because you are Jehovah God and nothing is impossible for you to do. You asked us, is my hand too short to save? Wherever your son is give us insight. Give us light where there is darkness, direct us where we do not know where to go, make our axe head float. Make it float. Make it float. Make it float. Make it float. Make it float.'

'Make it float' became a song, a rhythmic chant he intoned, eyes shut and feet stamping gently as he walked around the room, his voice rising, his head bobbing, his body swaying.

He stopped abruptly, whirled around on the balls of his feet and said 'My children, pray. Open your mouths and call on God. Let his light break through our darkness. Pray.'

As their prayers bubbled forth, the prophet's voice rose with every word uttered until he lapsed into tongues, stamping his feet and clapping in rhythm to his words.

It went on for about thirty minutes before he said a huge 'Praise the Lord' and all was quiet.

His white gown was drenched but there was on his face something almost beatific, a calm that seemed alien to the charged environment that had just been.

'I see our brother shrouded in darkness. We must do more. On Friday next week, we shall all gather here to pray and keep vigil. We will start at midnight and end at dawn. God will intervene.'

Auntie Ekwi thanked him. As they rose to go, she nudged Abel with a sharp elbow in the ribs. 'Find something for the prophet,' she whispered in Igbo.

Abel parted with the money in his pocket, which the prophet received with a 'God bless you, my son.'

They dropped Auntie Ekwi off at home in Ilupeju. Because Abel hadn't been to her house before and hadn't seen her husband since Soni's wedding, he stayed back to reacquaint himself with her two sons and talk about Soni and home and politics with her husband while Auntie Ekwi and Ada prepared lunch.

By the time they were done it was already past three. They drove in silence out of Ilupeju down to Town Planning Way and onto Ikorodu Road. Ada cruised past Obanikoro, Onipanu, Fadeyi and Jibowu, into Surulere.

Ojuelegba was busy, and as they slowed in the traffic leading to the bridge that would take them into Western Avenue, Abel felt someone tapping on the window beside him.

'Smoke, bros. Smoke,' a young man said, pointing to the hood.

'Ada, stop, stop. He says there is smoke coming out from the engine,' Abel said already reaching for the door lock. The young man was running alongside the car, pointing but Ada kept on driving.

'It's a trick, Abel. There is no smoke. If you stop, you are in trouble. Once you open your engine they will disconnect something and that's where it starts. You could get robbed or killed or made to part with some money.'

The young man, noticing that Ada wasn't slowing down, had stopped jogging alongside them. Abel saw him cross the road to wait for another hapless driver.

'First time it happened to me, I lost my handbag. I was lucky it was in the afternoon,' she said, slowing as she indicated right.

Back in the seventies, Fela had written a classic song about Ojuelegba. A concourse of sorts, it was a pure melee of cars, people and sounds. There were buses stopping in the middle of the road to pick up passengers, passengers jumping and falling off buses because the drivers would never come to a full stop to let off their fares, and in all that confusion traffic wardens were trying and failing to sanitise the madness and enforce some kind of order.

Things had improved a lot since then. The traffic lights worked, bus stops with roofed stalls had been built and Ojuelegba had become a tad gentrified, but it was still a part of Lagos, a place with a soul that gravitated towards the chaotic, an anarchic impulse that could never fully be tamed.

'Let's have some pepper soup. Do you mind?' she asked as she veered into the right lane, beside Teslim Balogun Stadium. 'They make really nice ones at O'jez and I haven't been here in a while.'

'O'jez. I thought it was in Yaba,' Abel said, recalling that, on his last visit to Lagos for Soni's wedding an old friend had taken him to a place called O'jez somewhere in Yaba.

'Yes, they were. They have a bigger place here.'

Ada turned left under the bridge beside the stadium. She waited for the road to clear then drove across into the National Stadium complex, past commuters massed around the bus stop. Men and women with muscular torsos and no legs pushed themselves along or simply lounged in pimped-out, hand-powered bikes and wheelchairs. A couple of them were smoking weed openly.

Ada drove slowly because of the speed bumps and Abel took in the rows of shops selling running shoes, swimming trunks, trophies and odd assortments of sports paraphernalia. They made a right and then she found a spot.

'Oya, come let me show you what it means to point and kill,' she said and there was trilling laughter in her voice.

As they walked into the rectangular enclosure, Abel noticed the rows of cars parked to the far left while two mobile policemen lounged in the shade with AK-47s slung across their knees.

'Why didn't you park inside?' Abel asked indicating the wide empty spaces.

'The car is safe outside and it is easier to leave. This is one of the safest places to hang out in Lagos.' They found a red table with four seats, all branded with the logo of a popular alcoholic beverage. To their right was a huge wall covered by a Visafone billboard, and underneath it was a screen showing music videos of Nigerian artistes.

'This place is a major hangout for Nigerian actors,' Ada told him. 'Come here often and you will meet all of them. They usually sit upstairs though.' She wiped their seats with a paper napkin. 'It doesn't fill up until around 7pm, when it gets dark. Soni used to say that's when people stroll in with women who are not their wives,'

'Like me,' Abel blurted out.

'Really?' Ada asked, the guardedness coming back.

'Don't mind me joo.' He forced a smile.

A slight Chinese lady in jeans and a sky blue top ambled over to their table, her face ablaze with a smile.

'Madam, how far?' she said, standing beside Ada. 'E don tay o, how oga dey?' she asked in unaccented pidgin.

'Oga travel, na im broda be dis.' Ada indicated Abel.

'Oga welcome,' she said, turning to Abel. 'Wetin una want.'

'Give us the 1,800 pepper soup,' Ada told her, then turned to Abel to ask what he wanted to drink.

'Big stout and a coke.'

'Give me Smirnoff Ice.'

'I go bring am now-now,' she said, and strode away.

'Is that woman Chinese?' Abel asked.

'No, she is from your village.' Ada smiled. 'The first time I met her, I was shocked too.'

'You guys come here often?'

'Yes. Soni always made time. Here and the movies; he made sure we came at least once a month. He liked the grilled fish and chips. Me, I prefer the pepper soup. Now, I am not sure whether I should have come. The memories are flooding in.'

'It's ok,' Abel said reaching out and touching her hand. It was the first time they'd had any kind of physical contact and he felt her pull back instinctively. 'You can't stay cooped up in that house forever.'

'I know, but it's hard sitting here waiting for pepper soup when Soni is not with me. I never came here without him, except when I brought my siblings.'

'What did you call him, my brother?'

'Why?'

'Just asking.'

'I called him Soni. What else should I call him? Honey?'

'No, not that. It's just that everyone calls him Sabato, even Auntie Ekwi and her husband.'

'I know. It was like a title and less a name; you know, something honorific. Soni used to laugh too when old schoolmates who

57

knew him as Kanayo or Soni would call him Sabato. He said he felt like they were showing him respect by not calling him by his real name. You know how, in Nigeria, once you become a governor, your friends stop calling you by your name and start calling you Excellency? That's how it was.'

'And you never caught the Sabato bug?'

'Me? Haba! I am his wife. I see him when he is not Sabato, when he sits in the loo, when he is prancing around naked, when he is goofing around with his son or fooling around in the house pretending to be Stevie Wonder on the piano. He is my baby, not Sabato.'

There was a faraway look in her eyes as she spoke and Abel could sense that whatever it was she had had with his brother, call it love or whatever, it had been deep.

'Oh, I forgot,' she said, returning to the present. 'I told you I would show you what point and kill is. Come.'

They walked to the right where the refrigerators were massed and the brightly liveried waiters picked up steaming bowls of pepper soup and cold drinks. Ada led him to a row of what appeared to be green glass walls, but on a closer look, Abel could see hundreds of fish swimming within.

'Oya, watch that couple,' Ada said.

Abel watched as a lady pointed and a guy on the other side of the tank dipped a metal basket-like utensil inside the tank and scooped up a catfish. He dropped it, gulping, on the table and, with one deft move, cracked its skull with a machete. The fish flapped about without purpose for a while then went still.

'You point and he kills,' Ada laughed.

'We have it in Asaba,' Abel said as they walked back to their table. 'But I have never seen so many fish.'

Their drinks had arrived by the time they returned and the pepper soup was delivered soon after.

'Head or tail?' Ada asked, indicating the two steaming bowls on the tray.

'You?' She pointed to the tail.

'Head it is then.'

THE SEDUCTIVE
MISTRESS

By spending time with Ada, whether dropping Zeal off at his summer kindergarten, eating pepper soup at O'jez, watching a movie at the cinema or going swimming at Ikoyi club, Abel was beginning to see a completely different side of Lagos. While it could be a city with a huge appetite for human flesh, it was also a seductive mistress with a tender touch.

True, the city had, like the hungry sea that bathed its haunches, opened its mouth wide and swallowed his brother whole, yet it was providing Abel with pleasures hitherto unexperienced, and it didn't hurt that he had a beautiful, intelligent woman for company.

On the days when he didn't go out to meet someone or see Edgar Ofio, the investigating police officer in charge of his brother's case, he would go to Ikoyi club with Ada. She loved to swim and even though there was a pool at the house she said she preferred to swim in the public pool.

'At least if you start drowning someone can help you,' she told him with a laugh. 'It's boring swimming alone.'

Abel could swim. He wasn't perfect but he had learnt, alongside his brother, from spending time at the village stream in his maternal homestead. That morning they had changed into their swimwear and were taking turns to stand under the tap before getting in the pool.

Ada had on a stunning one-piece swimsuit that accentuated her curves and hugged her bosom. Standing there, watching the water course all over her, Abel felt himself stir in an embarrassing way. He turned away quickly and placed his palm over his crotch.

They swam for a while and then he dried himself, pulled on a T-shirt, and left her at the pool to go and read the papers in the library. There, he came upon a story about a kidnap gang smashed by the police in Asaba. He was always tickled by the words journalists employed in such situations:

Robbery gang routed
Kidnap syndicate smashed
Robbery kingpin nabbed

You could almost predict the exact term, as if they had a bag of words they dipped into for certain reports.

The story about the four-man kidnap gang in Asaba made him think about home, or what used to be his home just one month ago. School would reopen in six weeks and he was glad he had finished marking his papers before he travelled. When he was leaving Asaba he had felt he would be gone for a couple of days at most, but a month and a few days later he was in Lagos living a completely new life.

There were luxury cars, a mansion, nice clothes, comfortable shoes, good food, a bar full of good wine and spirits – a life he couldn't have imagined two months back.

His brother was still missing, he knew, and even though he realised that hopes of ever finding his brother were growing dimmer with each passing day, he did not want to stop looking, aware that that was what was required of him. It was his duty as first son and older brother.

Steeling himself, Abel finally called their sister, Oby, and told her the bad news. While she sniffled and cried, he warned her not to tell their mother or relatives. He'd ensured that his mother's allowance was sent promptly, and when she'd called to ask after Soni, Ada told her that he was on a long trip to China.

Abel didn't know how long they could keep up the charade, but he knew that time always found a way to resolve even the thorniest issues.

He was duty-bound to do what was required of him as the first son and older sibling. He would search for his brother until it was clear that the search could no longer go on, and only then would he rest. When that time would come, however, he could not tell, and he did not know what he would do when the time came to go back to school.

Many nights as he lay in the downy bed, his head propped up by the softest pillows he had ever touched, Abel would wonder whether he could tear himself away from all this and return to his dump in Asaba. Could he go back to the drab, spartan life he used to live, away from the comfort of his brother's mansion, the times spent dining in nice restaurants and swimming at the club, his pocket bulging with money?

If he decided to quit his job, there was no fear of going broke, at least not in the foreseeable future. His brother had over eight hundred million naira in cash in six different banks. He had five houses in Lagos aside from the one he lived in and Ada told him there was an apartment in Essex and two in Florida.

'You know your brother can't stand the cold, so he had to buy a house in Florida, where the sun is always out.'

Abel's well-ordered but frugal life had suddenly been turned round. He was living the good life but existing in a state of flux. Was he now a Lagos Big Boy? Or a mere teacher on vacation?

These questions intruded upon him in his quiet moments. He always pushed them aside, but that morning, sitting in the small library at Ikoyi Club, Abel knew his future depended, in large part, on his ability to forget. Therein lay his dilemma: how to forget by not remembering.

How to sleep in a man's bed, how to get warm at the sight of his wife, how to wear his clothes, drink his wine, play with his son, spend his money and not remember that he was still missing.

The thought insisted upon an answer and left his eyes brimming with tears.

—

By the time Abel woke, the sun was up and there were strong rays streaming into his bed. He covered his face with a pillow to keep out the glare but he could still feel it hot against his skin. They hadn't got in until well past 6am, because they'd had to drop Auntie Ekwi at home. The vigil started at midnight and ran all the way to 5am. They sang and prayed; Abel, Auntie Ekwi, Ada and about a dozen prayer warriors enlisted for the vigil. The prophet and the prayer warriors spoke in tongues whenever the prophet asked them to pray in the Spirit.

Abel had wondered how he would cope, praying all night, but somehow the five hours had passed swiftly and he was surprised when the session came to an end and the prophet said his Alleluia.

This time, Abel was prepared with something substantial in an envelope.

'God will do it, my son,' the prophet told him as they filed out.

When he woke up that morning after napping for a few hours, he felt something else too – a stiffening of the joints. Pushing the pillow off, he tried to make a fist. It hurt. Alarm flooded him as he got off the bed. He walked naked to the bathroom to pass water, all the while trying tentatively to make a fist and feeling the pain shoot up his arm.

He was having an attack. He hadn't had one in about four years. He knew what medication was required, had always known since he was a kid, but the thought of it and the memories that came rushing in left him anxious.

He brushed his teeth, showered and got dressed. By the time he was done, he could hear Zeal laughing out loudly from behind the door in his mother's room. He had the same laughter Soni had, a high-pitched cackle full of joyful abandon. Abel marvelled at how the genes transferred even the most mundane things from father to son.

As he pulled on his socks, he glanced at the clock on the mantelpiece: 10.50am.

Downstairs, the house help was setting the table. She brought him the English breakfast Ada said Soni insisted on eating before he left the house every morning.

'Most times he eats once a day,' Ada had told him. 'And he always said one must eat like a king at breakfast.'

Abel had no appetite, so he drank coffee and nibbled at the toast.

He drove out of the compound, his mind on Victoria Island. He was headed to a pharmacy on the ground floor of the Silverbird Galleria. Ada had taken him there once after a movie to buy Vitamin C and cold remedies for Zeal.

'At least here you can be sure of what you are buying,' Ada had said. 'Most people die in this country not from poor care, but from fake drugs, do you know that?' She had a way of ensuring that you responded by asking a question at the end of her comment.

Abel said he thought so. An aunt of theirs, the one who came before his mum, had died from a fake dose. She had survived a motor accident and was prescribed an anti-tetanus injection on account of her injuries. Abel's dad had gone to buy it because it was not stocked at the local hospital where she had been admitted. He ended up buying a fake dose. She got lockjaw and died four days later.

'My father was devastated and never forgave himself. In so many ways, I felt as if he loved that woman, Auntie Ify, more than he loved my mum. It was through her that he met my mother, and her death was something he never got over. My mum told me he went to the chemist where he bought the drugs and beat up the owner. He was arrested but, according to my mum, my father would have gladly gone to the gallows just to make it right.'

'Wow, Soni never told me that story.'

'We were quite young. I was four or five and Soni must have been two or three. I'm sure he didn't remember.'

'Well, you know what they do to people who sell fake drugs in China?'

Abel shook his head.

'They execute them; one bullet to the head. If they did that in Lagos, many people would die.'

'It's that bad, eh?' Despite his aunt, who had died many years ago in that remote village, he hadn't really thought there was an epidemic of fake drugs. The ones he bought were mostly for headache or diarrhoea or they were antimalarials. They were everywhere and he had never taken any that weren't effective. When his attacks came, he knew what cocktail to take and it had always worked from the time he was in the boarding house right through university.

'It is. I remember just after Zeal was born. We were still living at Ilupeju then. I asked the driver to buy baby food and he went to a shop close by instead of the supermarket we usually bought from. That night, Zeal started stooling. It was crazy. By 5am when we eventually braved it and drove out to the hospital he was as light as a piece of paper. They had to pass a line and Soni was crying and vowing to kill somebody if his son died. I couldn't stop teasing him afterwards but there and then, as I watched my son wither before my eyes, I could have killed someone too.

When we got back, Soni had the driver take him there. He reported the shop to the police and got NAFDAC involved. When the man was arrested, all he kept saying was "because you have money, abi, because you have money". He didn't see that he had almost killed a baby. They should do the China thing here – one bullet to the head.' She pointed a cocked finger at her temple.

Abel's thoughts were everywhere as he drove past the tollgate, onto Ozumba Mbadiwe, and sped past the impressive Oriental Hotel, which everyone said was owned by a past governor of Lagos state.

He took a left turn at the Civic Centre – owned by Jim Ovia, former banker and one of Africa's richest men – into Adetokunbo Ademola. The 1004 Estate was to his left. He remembered visiting a friend once, back when he was at university. He had been disappointed. The place was dirty, crowded and filled with cars, most of them broken down. Inside, the houses didn't look too impressive either. There was a pervasive civil-service air about the place that spoke of neglect.

It had been built in a fit of indulgence and excess by the federal government as residential quarters for 1004 federal legislators – hence the name. They stayed for a while and then, like all things Nigerian, it was no longer used for its true purpose. A coup took place and suddenly there were no more senators or legislators and the seat of government moved to Abuja, the new federal capital.

So, it became an estate where lucky civil servants and even some non-civil servants who had Godfathers could live.

It was purpose-built, well-appointed and beautifully laid out, but with time, all that changed and the estate lost its allure. Things were changing again. The government had sold the estate to private investors who had renovated it. New tenants were moving in and it was no longer as crowded as it used to be. Abel and Ada had gone there to visit a lady a few days back. There were guards at the gates and the estate looked a whole lot better than it had years ago when he first visited.

'That's where the guy landed when he jumped,' Ada said, pointing to a concrete slab stained brown. She had been telling him a story of a murder/suicide.

'What happened to that case?'

'Nothing,' Ada said, shaking her head. 'Open and shut.'

The story was that a young woman who ran a nightclub had been attacked by a man who worked for her and whom the tabloids said might also have been her lover.

She was attacked viciously but had managed to call for help. By the time security guards rushed in however, the supposed lover had jumped off the sixth-floor ledge and landed on the slab.

Abel remembered reading the story in the weekend papers back in Asaba and not hearing anything again. What he hadn't realised was that Lagos was like that. In a city with over fifteen million people seemingly always in a mad rush to get some place fast, nothing held your attention for too long. It was that way with everything: nightclubs, schools, banks, estates, cars, scandals.

Everything had a season.

He drove the length of Adetokunbo Ademola, past the imposing Eko Hotel and Suites, before making a right turn at Bar Beach then driving all the way down Ahmadu Bello Way to the Silverbird Galleria. Because it was a Saturday, mothers supported by an army of house helps were herding their children into the Galleria to shop and see movies.

Most people worked on the Island, where a lot of the companies and banks were clustered. The factories, shipping lines and other businesses engaged in production and distribution were spread out farther afield, some in Apapa (because of its proximity to the ports) but mostly on the mainland all over the Ikeja, Ilupeju, Agidingbi, Ogba and Apapa axes.

Most of those who worked on the Island lived on the mainland and had to commute from areas as far flung as Ikorodu, Sango Ota and Egbeda. To beat the energy-sapping traffic they left home early, meaning that some parents never got to see their children awake during the week. Saturdays became days for making up and were almost as busy as the weekdays, with people shopping, going to the movies, the beach or to weddings. People tried to pack into Saturdays all the things they couldn't do from Monday to Friday. Sundays were reserved for church services in a city that, though amoral and riddled with crime and criminals, also paraded some of the most ardent churchgoers.

Abel parked the car and walked into the Galleria. He was stopped and searched.

'What's that beeping in your pocket?' the guard asked, running his hand over his right thigh.

Abel pulled back, reached inside and brought out the gold-plated pen he'd picked up from Soni's dresser.

'We didn't have these searches before,' Ada had told him the first time they came to the movies. 'But with Boko Haram, no one is taking chances.'

Inside, Abel found the drugs he needed. He bought a bottle of water and downed six tablets, then left the pharmacy and took the elevator upstairs. He went into the bookshop and cruised the aisles, browsing through the titles before picking up a copy of Toni Morrison's *Sula*. He thought the price was a bit steep but decided to buy it anyway. He had owned a copy once, but an ex-girlfriend had borrowed and never returned it. The first day he met her, he told her she reminded him of Sula.

'Who is she?' she had asked, oblivious.

'It's a character in a book.'

'I remind you of a character in a book? How is that possible? Characters in books are not real people,' she'd said, half-amused, half-intrigued.

'I will lend you the book to read and if she doesn't remind you of yourself, you can call me a liar.'

It was one of his best pick-up lines and he knew Soni would have been impressed. They were lovers for two years, then she left town and they lost contact.

He paid for the book and was taking the stairs down when he heard his name.

'Abel Dike!' It was a female voice and there was some tentativeness to it.

Abel turned round and screamed, 'Calista Adeyemi!'

'It's a lie!' she cried as they hugged. 'Where did you fall out from?'

'Asaba,' he said, smiling and giddy with joy.

'What are you doing in Lagos? You finally left Asaba, have you?' She guided him downstairs to a fast-food restaurant. They found a seat and, laughing like the young girl he used to know, she took his hands in hers and whispered like a shy schoolgirl, 'I have missed you, Mister Dike.'

'And me, you,' he replied and meant it.

They had gone out for three years back at university and he remembered how Soni would tease him: 'Bros, so you are going to fuck only one girl in this school?'

They'd lived together for two years, then split after graduation, when she had gone abroad for her master's. He had refused to marry her and become a British citizen.

'You broke my heart so badly I am still picking up the pieces,' she said. Calista had always been direct and open about her feelings.

'I'm sorry, but I was too young and you were just too focused.'

He held her gaze for a while. A smile danced around the edges of her full lips. She hadn't changed much, even though age had given her face more character. She still had the dimple in one cheek, the twinkle in her eyes and the crow's feet that appeared when she smiled. Her teeth were still as white and even as he remembered them, and deep in her eyes he could see that she still had it for him.

'So, how many kids do you have now?' he asked

'None, yet. You?'

'None. I haven't found someone to marry me. You married?'

She shook her head. 'Nope. You used me up. You left nothing of value.'

He heard her laugh and was transported to the University of Jos, to the cramped space he shared with Soni and one other student before he and Calista moved in together. It was a Friday morning and they were making love and for some reason she was having these multiple orgasms and she always had the giggles whenever she came. It went on and on and suddenly there was a banging on the door. Abel ignored it at first but the person was insistent, so he asked who it was.

'It's Rahman.' His Muslim neighbour.

'What's up, Rahman?' Abel asked. 'You need the iron?'

'No. It's Ramadan and I am fasting, please.'

They had stopped, but whenever either of them felt like making love they would say, 'I am fasting, please.' It became a sort of code.

'So, what brings you to Lagos?'

'My brother is missing.'

'What, 9 Inches?'

'Yes, the same one.'

'Sorry to hear that. What happened?'

He filled her in as fast as he could. He was tired of telling the story.

'That's so sad. I work for the Lagos State Government in the governor's office. If you come by, I could introduce you to the CSO. Maybe he can help with the police. The police always need to be prodded, you know.'

'Thanks,' Abel said, wondering how, just sitting there and talking to her, it didn't feel as if there had been a ten-year hiatus.

'So, you came to see a movie?' she asked.

'No. I came to buy my drugs. My knuckles were hurting when I woke up this morning.'

'Really, you still have those?' She had seen him through more than a dozen episodes back in school.

'Yes, but not as often as I used to. I haven't had one in four years but I suspect the stress is finally getting to me.'

'If you are free, we could drive down to my place. I stay at 1004. I can make you jollof rice and smoked fish.'

'You still remember?' he asked, and she smiled a knowing smile.

They walked out together and drove to her place, Abel following her Kia Sportage SUV. She lived in one of the duplexes. The interior was simple, minimal but colourfully done up in pastels.

'You want a drink while I cook?' she called from the kitchen but Abel didn't answer. Instead he walked up to her, enfolded her from behind and said 'I thought you were fasting.'

There was the briefest pause as her brows furrowed, then she smiled in remembrance as she turned to kiss him, standing on tiptoe like she used to. He kissed her back, his body responding to her like it hadn't to anyone else in years.

'Show me your bed,' he said, nibbling on her ears, and she led him upstairs, like a lamb to its shearers.

Lying naked afterwards, her head on his shoulders, her breath warm against his skin, Abel remembered the first time she had found him sick, curled up on the floor of his room, his knuckles aching, his body burning up.

She had pulled him onto his mattress. He told her what the issue was and that even though he had felt the pains in his joints the day before, he didn't have money to buy his drugs.

'What are they called?' she asked. 'I can borrow some money from my cousin.'

He gave her the names, and after making sure that he would be OK, she raced out of Village Hostels, took a bike to town and returned in less than an hour.

'I've had it since I was five years old,' he explained later, as the drugs brought relief.

'At first they thought it was sickle cell, but my parents were both AA. It turned out that it was just some genetic glitch. There's no cure, although the specialist who diagnosed it said attacks would get less frequent as I got older.'

'Can you pass it on to our kids?' she asked, straddling him.

'It's possible.' He felt himself stir. 'Won't you let a sick guy rest?'

'I will. Just relax; I'll do all the work.' She laughed as she took him in her hand.

Lying there in her bed, he remembered how sick he used to get as a child. He couldn't exert himself, which meant there was no football and before they finally found out what it was and what drugs they could use to suppress it, Abel lost two years of school, with Soni catching up to him. They had ended up finishing primary and secondary school as well as university at the same times.

His ill health affected everything. He was weak, he didn't have friends, he couldn't drink beer, didn't smoke and found it hard to get a girlfriend because he always felt self-conscious. What if the girl found him all contorted and sick? Would she stay? Would she come back?

Calista had found him and she had come back and she had stayed. For that he was grateful.

He eased up a bit and kissed her on the forehead.

'What was that for?' she asked, her eyes fluttering open.

'For being you, my darling.'

———

He had six missed calls from Ada.

He had left his phone in the car when they got to Calista's and Ada had been calling. The house help had told her he was sick and she was worried when he didn't come back on time. She had also sent a text message: *Philo told me you were not feeling well and we are worried you haven't come back. Did you have an attack? Soni told me about it. Please call.*

He didn't call. He sent a message saying he was OK and on his way home.

'Are you alright?' she asked, jumping to her feet when he walked in.

'I am good.' Zeal ran straight into his arms.

'So where did you go all this while?'

'I went to get my drugs, then ran into an old friend and we went to her house.'

'You were with a woman all this while and I have been worried out of my head,' she snapped. Abel looked up, startled by her tone. She was standing there, tears in her eyes and a pained look on her face.

'Ada, I forgot my phone in the car. I'm sorry.' He reached out to touch her but she jumped back.

'You and your brother – you guys won't kill me. You hear? I haven't found my husband and you want me to go looking for his brother. Please give me my son and you can go back to your lady friend.'

She snatched Zeal out of his hands and ran upstairs while Abel stared open mouthed after her.

He slept for a few hours. When he awoke, he washed his face and rinsed his mouth before walking downstairs. As he went down the winding staircase, lines from Eliot came to mind.

And indeed there will be time
To wonder, "Do I dare?" and, "Do I dare"

Back at Unijos, he had a friend, Olu, who could recite the whole poem. They would go to the Law Faculty with its winding staircase and Olu would intone the lines with Abel jumping in on occasion as they walked all the way down, as if tracing Eliot's trajectory.

Downstairs at the house, the aroma of jollof rice filled his nostrils and made his stomach grumble. In the kitchen, Ada was stirring the rice in the pot.

'Do you feel better?' she asked, making it less awkward for him.

She must have been swimming because she had on a silk robe. It was slightly parted at the top to reveal ample cleavage.

'Yes,' he said, then added, 'I'm sorry about earlier ...'

'It's OK.' She raised a palm to stop him, her robe falling open some more. 'I think I overreacted. Why don't you wait by the deck? Zeal is playing in the pool. This should be ready in minutes. I'm sure you are hungry.'

'Yes, thanks,' Abel said and turned to go. He was crossing the living room when she called his name. 'Yes, Ada?'

'Red wine or beer?' She stood framed against the door, looking ravishing with her half-open robe, dishevelled hair and pose.

'Beer will do, with the food.'

Zeal was pottering about in his own side of the pool with Philo keeping an eye on him.

'Uncle Abel!' he cried. Abel stooped beside him and sprayed water in his face. When the water hit him, Zeal laughed that same high-pitched laugh that Abel knew so well, right from when they were kids into adulthood. Soni laughed at the silliest things and at the most inappropriate times.

Once, they had been given a ride by his father's colleague, the vice principal admin. Soni and Abel were sitting in the back with the man's daughter while his son sat in front. A song came on the radio and appeared to be one the man liked. He started singing along, but there was a problem. Each time the word 'sunshine' was sung, the man would say 'sunchine' and Soni would laugh. Abel would poke him in the ribs to stop but the more he poked him the more he laughed. Everyone was embarrassed, except for the man, who didn't realise why Soni was laughing.

When the song ended, he turned back to look at them and asked, 'What was so funny?' Any normal child would have shaken his head and said nothing or told some lie, but not Soni.

'Because you kept saying "sunchine"' Soni said, and burst into laughter.

The man stepped on the brakes, pulled open the car door and threw them out.

Their father was so upset with the man for letting his children trek home, they never spoke again, but it was Soni whom Abel blamed, even though no one else did.

'He is an adult for God's sake. He should control his temper,' their mother had said as she fussed over Soni.

'Carry me,' Zeal cried as Abel straightened.

'How long has he been here?' he asked the help as he reached in to pull Zeal up.

'Over one hour,' she informed him as he swaddled Zeal in the towel she had provided.

He set him on his lap as he took off his wet swimming gear, then tickled him as he dressed him in dry clothes.

'If you stay in water too long you will become a fish,' Abel told him.

'I want to be a fish,' he said pulling at Abel's moustache. 'It's like Daddy's.' he said, and Ada, who was bringing the food, almost tripped.

'He keeps referring to him these days. He has been doing that since Monday.'

'It is good. A son should not forget his father,' Abel said as he picked up his plate of steaming food. From as far back as he could remember, jollof rice and smoked fish had been his favourite meal. 'I love jollof rice,' he told Ada as he dug in.

'I know, Soni told me. I cooked this as a peace offering,' she said as she too began to eat.

Abel hadn't realised how hungry he was until he swallowed the first mouthful. After making love at Calista's, they had lain in bed and drifted off to sleep, forgetting all about the food she had promised to make for him.

'Is there anything Soni did not tell you?'

'About you?'

Abel nodded. He poured his beer and took a sip.

'He talked about you all the time. I used to wonder what it was about you. I didn't like you and if you were my brother I would have hated you because it seemed you set a pretty high standard.'

'You hated me already,' Abel blurted.

'Yes, I know, and it wasn't exactly my fault. You didn't make it easy to like you.'

'And now?' he asked, treading softly, fishing to see whether what he felt and sensed was mutual.

'And now what, Mr Dike?' she asked, feigning seriousness even though her eyes were laughing.

'You still hate me?'

'Yes, hard enough to go half mad when I didn't see you.'

'Sorry.'

'Please, stop saying sorry. I overreacted. I suppose I am getting, you know, used to you being around and I just panicked. And then to find out you were with another woman … I just, you know …' She went back to her food.

Abel changed the topic. 'You know, when you talk about Soni like that, I find it hard to believe, sometimes. It's as if you are talking about someone else, not the same Soni I grew up with. I always assumed I was the one trying to measure up to him. Everything came easy to him. Any time we moved to a new town or school people gravitated towards him. I always considered myself a failure. Yes, I wanted to be a vice principal, but see what I ended up as.'

'You have something, you know? You talk to people and it's like they have to listen. Soni used to say that every reprimand from you was like a whiplash.'

'He did?' She nodded. 'And yet the idiot never listened to me.'

'But he did. He almost didn't marry me because he felt you disapproved.'

'Now I know why you were pissed off with me.'

'Yes, now you know,' she laughed. 'One day, he was talking to me and he said "See, I am here in Lagos trying to make it, you know, to be a wealthy man. But Abel, he is just content being a teacher. I don't see him under any pressure. I want to be like that, you know, but I am wired differently."'

'He told you that?'

'Yes. He also said that you never needed to … how did he put it now? Swim against the currents because the currents flowed along with you.'

'And do you believe him?'

'Yes, I do. You look content, and contentment is important for happiness.'

'I have my own issues, Ada, my own neuroses. The pig sweats but we don't notice because of the hair.'

'I wish we were all that hairy.'

Abel laughed. 'You are hairy enough,' he said, pointing. Her robe had fallen open, her swimsuit had shifted and tufts of pubic hair were visible.

'Onye ala!' she cried, snapping her legs shut.

O BROTHER, WHERE ART THOU?

Lying in bed later that night, Abel thought about what she had told him. He had considered Soni a rival; someone he had to battle for everything: their parents' love and affection, academic achievement, sporting prowess, friends, girls, right from when they were kids.

It got worse after he lost two years to illness and they ended up as classmates. Abel was smarter, no doubt, but who needed smarts when you were kids?

What he'd wanted most was to be a boy like Soni. Abel wanted to break a leg or an arm, stub a toe, sustain a cut; something that would require him coming to school with his hand in a sling, his foot in a cast or a plaster on his face. He hankered after a badge of courage, something that would mark him, scar him, show that he was a boy – for what was a boy without scars?

Back then, a fracture was the coolest injury a boy could have. It signified boyhood because who ever heard of a girl with a fracture? A fracture required a cast and a cast meant people would beg to write or draw or inscribe something on it. As a moving billboard, you attracted everyone, especially the girls.

But, most of all, a fracture meant one had been boy enough to break something.

But for a child who played more in the library than on treetops, a fracture was not likely unless he hurled himself down the steps leading to the huge doors of their local Catholic church; a thought that occurred to him many times.

Soni had no such issues. Their parents spent a lot on plasters, slings and casts. As soon as one was healing, Soni was acquiring a fresh badge of courage. Abel couldn't help but be impressed and jealous.

It continued at the University of Jos, where Soni went about without boxers and, it seemed, a constant hard-on. Abel thought it was insane and stupid but the girls didn't seem to mind. Soni ran through them like fire through hay and never forgot to leave his calling card above their beds: *9 inches was here.*

Abel still remembered the last time they'd had a fight. It was Easter and he had just been paid his first salary, a measly fifty-three thousand naira. He had planned to send his mother some money, then buy a bigger mattress, but a call came in from Lagos and messed everything up.

Soni was in jail and had sent for him.

Abel took the night bus from Onitsha and arrived Lagos the next morning. It was a Wednesday morning and Ojota, where the bus let him off, was a mess. It had rained the night before and the ground was soggy and unsightly. Bedlam did not begin to capture the situation. Cars were revving and people were shouting as if in competition: hawkers belting out their wares, conductors calling out their destinations, itinerant pastors preaching about repentance, hell and damnation. Abel hadn't spent five minutes in the city and he was already feeling he had stayed too long. It seemed as if a million people had descended on Ojota with one purpose: to make him feel unwelcome.

Soni was being held at Area F in Ikeja, so Abel boarded a bus at Ojota that would take him to Maryland. He alighted at the Mobil filling station and took another bus to Ikeja roundabout. They stopped at Unity bus stop to let off a female passenger. Two guys transporting metal roofing sheets were passing by as she stepped out of the bus. The edge of the sheets hit her, slicing off a piece of her forehead. Blood coursed down her face.

The conductor pushed her back in the bus and they sped off to the General Hospital. By the time Abel got off, her white blouse was drenched with blood and she was already feeling faint.

He took a bike to Area F and asked for the investigating police officer handling his brother's case. His name was Sergeant Ilo. The policeman was in mufti and had on a tight, ill-fitting jacket. As Abel watched him shuffling papers in an exaggerated show of importance, he smiled to himself for the first time since he got his brother's text message: if the policeman's jacket was any tighter it would be a strait jacket.

'Your brother's case is serious,' the policeman began when he finally sat down across from Abel.

The cramped excuse of an office reeked of sweat and deprivation. There were tattered files, cobwebbed corners, a rickety table and a chair missing a leg, but above all there was a pervasive spirit of desolation, of something irretrievably lost. Abel cursed his brother for making him go there.

'It's a case of OBT,' the officer said, all solemn, as if he was a judge about to hand down a death sentence.

'What's OBT?'

'You don't know what OBT is?' He went on without waiting for an answer. 'What do you do for a living?'

'I am a teacher; a lecturer.'

'Where, what school?'

'College of Education, Asaba.'

'You are a teacher and you don't know what OBT is, so what do you teach your students?'

'English literature,' Abel said and laughed, amused by it all. Why on earth was he supposed to know what OBT was and what did that have to do with his job or students?

'You think it's funny, abi? OK, go home and come back tomorrow.' The officer got to his feet and headed for the door.

'Haba, officer, I was just joking. No vex.' Abel got up and stood between the policeman and the door. 'Please sit down, OK. I don't know what OBT is but I am sure you will help us, abeg no vex.'

The policeman regarded Abel for a while, his brow furrowed, like a child contemplating an insect crawling vainly up a steel surface. Then he went back to his seat.

'Your brother tried to obtain funds by tricks from someone,' he said finally. 'He was arrested and brought here. You are lucky the woman does not want to press charges, but we can't just let him go. He has been our guest for three nights now and he has enjoyed our hospitality. Someone has to pay for that, you know?'

'I understand. What are we looking at?'

'Obtaining By Tricks is a major issue right now,' the policeman began, shuffling the files again. 'You know, 419 has messed up our image abroad so government is not taking issues of fraud lightly, even though OBT is local. With one hundred thousand naira, you can get him out,' he said and slammed the files back on the table.

One hundred thousand naira; that was his salary for two months, but he didn't let on. Instead he said, 'You know he is a first-time offender. You guys should treat him better.'

They haggled for a while and settled for twenty-five thousand, which was all the money he had on him, save three thousand naira he kept for his fare back.

Soni was smiling when he came out of the cell. He wore his shirt and trousers inside out.

'Bros, no vex,' he said with a giggle as he passed Abel.

Right there, in that dank corridor with its clammy floor that sucked at your feet as if unwilling to let you go, that corridor that reeked of sweat and piss and shit and an unusual cocktail of foulness, Abel watched open-mouthed as his brother took off his trousers in front of a policewoman who was passing by them, his manhood dangling long and free as usual. He watched him turn the trousers out the right way before putting them back on.

After he had done the same with his shirt, Abel trailed him to the counter, where Soni signed a sheet and was handed his wristwatch and bracelet.

'Where is my ring?' Soni asked, but the female police officer who had walked past them earlier just glowered at him.

'Get out of here, mister man! Was it your mother that has been cleaning the toilet for you?'

Outside, Soni said he was hungry and they walked to the far end of the station, where a wooden shack sat like an outhouse. He ordered food, asking for three pieces of meat.

'I have just three thousand naira left,' Abel told him, fighting hard to keep his temper in check, rattled as he was by his brother's insouciant air. Soni said it was OK and settled on a bench.

He ate with an appetite and Abel was struck by the thought that, if someone walked in and saw them, that person would assume Abel was the reason why they were at a police station. Soni did not seem to have a care.

The meal over and paid for, Soni stood up and motioned for his brother to come with him. He hailed a cab and negotiated a fare of one thousand naira to his place on Opebi, off Salvation Road.

The place they went up to was a cute, self-contained, one-bedroom apartment with a toilet and kitchen. It was clean and furnished all in black, from the bedspread to the rug and couch.

'Welcome to my humble abode,' Soni said as Abel settled into the settee. Then he ran out to go pay the waiting taxi driver. When he returned, Abel watched him undress and step into the bathroom. 'You can put on the TV. You can watch CNN,' Soni shouted.

Showered, dressed and relaxed, he sat on the bed opposite his brother. 'Abel, I am sorry, but there was no one else to call.'

'You have to stop this, Soni,' Abel said, the frustration of the past two days, the money he had lost, the time he had wasted, the whole pot of complaints boiling over as a frothing lava of angry words. 'Find a decent job. Look at you; what is this? You are now a common criminal. You need to find a decent job.' Abel told him, all the pent up rage coming to the fore.

'What job, Abel? Teaching? Wearing a tie to work in a bank? Is that the job you want me to find?' Soni raged. 'Do you know what people who don't have godfathers do to get bank jobs? They fuck some of the girls in the toilet before the interviews. The toilet, Abel. Is that what you want from me, to sleep with old women so I can get deposits or work as a teacher and earn something that won't be enough to rent a decent place? Is that what you want? Penury for all of us, like you?'

Abel lashed out to slap him. Soni grabbed his hand mid-air and was throwing a punch when he stopped himself.

'Next time they arrest you, don't call me. Call your rich friends.' Abel snatched his hand away and reached for his bag. He was at the door when Soni's voice stayed his feet.

'Bros, please don't go. Stop, please.' Soni reached for his brother's bag, snapping the strap in the process.

'I have no rich friends, Abel. You are all I have. See.' He pulled up his mattress and opened a secret compartment in the bed.

'I have about a million naira here. If I sent someone, I would never see the money again. If I came home with the police, they would steal it. You were the only one I could call and I thought that when you got to Area F I would tell you where I kept it. I didn't realise you would have the money. I am sorry but you are my big brother, Abel, the only one I can run to.'

Soni was crying now and Abel held him close, his own eyes burning with unshed tears.

When he had calmed down, Abel helped him count the money. He took out what he had spent and told Soni to open a bank account.

With the cash in the travel bag he had emptied, they trekked through a shortcut to Opebi road right behind the Sheraton Hotel and deposited the money in a savings account. It was Soni's first ever bank account.

THIS IS LAGOS

They were on their way to Ikeja. Santos was driving and Abel was riding shotgun. They had three appointments that Monday morning and had left the house early.

First they needed to see the lawyer, then Matthew Chu, some Chinese man in Gbagada who Santos said handled Soni's imports from China. Finally, they had to meet with one of Soni's account officers. She had called Santos to say she needed to talk to Abel about Soni's account.

The first meeting went well. The lawyer had found a co-operative judge who said he could grant a probate injunction allowing limited access to the accounts so long as Abel and Ada agreed to act as co-signatories and administrators of Soni's estate, pending his return or proof of death.

'It will take us about ten to fourteen days to prepare the document and regularise it, but after that we can have access,' the lawyer explained as he walked them to the car.

Matthew, the Chinese agent, wasn't around but he called while they were waiting at his office to say that three containers had arrived from China for Soni and the customers who usually bought the goods from them were on standby.

He invited Abel over to his club on Friday to sign some documents since his powers as next of kin had been effected. Chu said it was his treat and that he needed the documents signed because he was leaving for Taiwan the next day. Abel asked Santos where the club was and if it was a good idea to go; Santos said it was.

'Bros, you can't miss that club o. Na the best strip joint for Lagos mainland be dat o. Bros Santos dey go dia sometimes especially when e get visitors.'

They left the Gbagada office and drove all the way down, past Charly Boy bus stop, past the Mobil filling station and on to the overpass that took them back towards Anthony Village.

As they descended, Abel turned to Santos and pointed out the window. 'That's the road to Deeper Life Church, right?'

'Yes, bros. You know person for that side?'

Abel shook his head as memories washed over him. He had walked those dusty streets many years back. He'd been spending his long vacation in Lagos with a friend, at the end of his first year at Unijos. Back then, Gbagada was not so developed. A friend's older brother had just returned from the US and asked them to look for a befitting house for him, with the promise of a good commission. Their search had led Abel and his friend, Moses, to Obasa Street, close to a development that would, years later, become the gated community of Medina Estate. They found a lovely four-bedroom apartment, but his friend's parents didn't like the location. They said Gbagada was undeveloped and got him a house in Oshodi instead.

A few years later, when Abel visited another friend in Gbagada, he was amazed at how things had changed. Gbagada had become a trendy area while Oshodi had regressed. That was a huge surprise, a lesson in how poor judgement could make all the difference when it came to real estate.

Santos turned off the expressway into Anthony Village through an imposing gate that led past Newcastle Hotel and Sherlaton restaurant so he could avoid the traffic ahead. He meandered through the many tight corners and side streets that made up Anthony Village, a semi-upscale locale that, despite its somnolence, was or had been home to some of the hottest activists the country had known, from people's lawyer, Gani Fawehinmi to his acolyte, Festus Keyamo as well as Beko Ransome-Kuti, the medical doctor and younger brother of Afrobeat legend Fela Kuti.

They had just made it past the building that housed the designer Mudi, and had turned right to head towards Maryland when they ran into the traffic gridlock Santos had been trying to avoid.

'Kai,' Santos cried. 'Lagos traffic is like evil spirit.'

They waited for close to ten minutes before the cars in front began to move but the two directly ahead of them remained stationary. Santos tapped on his horn twice, then turned to Abel. 'Bros, put that bag under your seat o, they may be armed robbers.'

Santos tried to reverse but the car behind was too close. He wound down the window and motioned for the guy to ease off but the man motioned back to say there was a car right behind him.

By now, car horns were blaring, so a passer-by went to the man in the car upfront to see what the problem was. He staggered back and began to scream.

'The man is dead. E don die o.'

Santos killed the engine and he and Abel stepped out. The man was slumped over and lying halfway into the front passenger seat, the seat belt holding him up. Santos poked him, but there was no response and by now a crowd had gathered and people were screaming and speaking all at once.

Santos and Abel made it back to the vehicle and Santos managed to manoeuvre the car out of the jam. They rode off, past the man dead in his car, swallowed whole by Lagos, like many before him.

At the bank, Nicole, the lady they had come to see, was not in the building but she had left a message for them to wait, so Abel and Santos sat in the banking hall.

It was one of the new generation banks that Abel had once heard a wag describe as 'boutique banks'. Architectural statements, their decor were always top notch and, walking into the banking halls, one had the feeling of walking into the reception area of a five-star hotel.

Abel could still remember the days of Progress Bank and Savannah Bank, when the big banks were just First, Union and the old UBA, and their receptions looked like glorified market stalls.

In those days, a bank was a place you went to when you were sure there was nothing urgent because you almost always ended up spending the whole day waiting to cash a cheque.

Now, it was all different and sitting in the banking hall, looking at the pretty, well-turned-out girls in the glass booths, you didn't feel like going anywhere in a hurry.

When a booth was free, the pretty girl in the counter motioned at Abel. He smiled and waved to say no, I am not here to withdraw or make a deposit.

His phone vibrated and he dug in his pocket to fish it out. It was a text message from Calista.

Hey Mister Dike, r u still coming 2 Alausa?
Do u want to see me?
sure, silly, where r u @
In ikeja. Waiting at the bank to see my brother's account officer.
a lady?
Yes
she pretty?
Haven't met her before. Why do you ask?
curious.
Curious? Remember what killed the cat?
yes. Buzz when u r done. Got news 4 u.
Sure

By the time Abel put his phone off and looked up a scene was playing out.

'You know me, right? Don't you know me?'

A thickset woman in jeans and a T-shirt with an electric air of menace around her was standing in front of the pretty customer-care officer. Her voice was loud and her gestures were aggressive.

The girl was sitting down but there was fear in her eyes and it was obvious that she wanted to be anywhere but there.

'How may I help you, ma?' she asked again and the woman slapped her. It was a hard slap that knocked her off her seat.

'You have helped me enough, *ashewo*. You have helped me enough by fucking my husband, you prostitute.'

The woman was screaming now and towering over the girl, who was crying.

'Security. Call security,' someone yelled, just as Abel sprang to his feet and walked towards her.

'Madam,' he said, reaching out to touch the woman, who whirled round and gave him a withering look.

'Oga, mind your business,' she said and reached for the bag she had dropped on the table.

Abel stepped back, thinking that it was all done. From the corner of his eye he could see two security men approaching.

What happened next would stay imprinted on his mind forever.

The woman picked up the bag, pulled out a yellow plastic container that had once contained custard powder, unscrewed the cap and threw the contents at the young woman, who was still struggling to get up from the floor.

'Acid!' Abel heard someone scream as the girl cried out, but it was not acid. It was something worse, something more shameful, more atavistic – a throwback to an ancient shaming ritual: she had bathed the young woman with shit.

The banking hall was a mad house. The stink was suffocating and the security men couldn't approach as she brandished the container like a weapon.

It was a sight to behold. The guards shouting at her to drop it, the young girl screaming as she tore her clothes off, the woman cursing and raging with righteous indignation, her tirade punctuated with screams of 'ashewo', as if the epithet was the sad refrain to an angry song.

Finally, a mobile police officer entered with a gun and threatened to shoot. That was when she let the container drop and broke down in tears.

'Bros na wa o,' Santos kept saying when he finally found his tongue. 'That woman just mad. Kai, see what she did to that fine girl. Na too much love dey make woman crase like dis.'

Abel looked at him and wondered whether Santos could not also see that the young girl had done something to hurt the woman. It was neither visible nor physical but it had cut to the bone. You needed to have been pushed to your limits to plan such an audacious attack.

'Anger is not a nice thing,' Abel told him as they were herded upstairs to wait so the banking hall could be cleaned and refreshed.

Nicole was all smiles as she walked into the waiting room to meet them.

She was a stunner; pretty in an understated way. There wasn't a part of her that stood out but everything added up; her pretty face, her well-cut skirt, the long legs accentuated by high heels, hips that fanned out into a nice derrière and a smile that lit up the room.

'I am Dr Nicole,' she said.

'Dr Nicole?' Abel asked, not sure he had heard right.

'Yes. UBTH. Class of 2004.' She smiled, flashing perfect rows of teeth.

'So what are you doing in a bank?' Abel asked, charmed. She was the kind of woman you didn't want to stop talking to, the kind you didn't want to let go her hand.

'Survival. Money. Doctors don't have it as good as they used to. Please come with me. Santos, please give us a few minutes.'

She preceded Abel into a cubicle marked 'Head of Operations' and pushed a tray of sweets towards him. Abel shook his head.

'Thank you for coming,' she told him and Abel smiled. 'I sent you that text,' she said matter-of-factly.

'Which one?'

'Soni is missing.' I knew you would come. Soni told me once that if he ever got into trouble, there was only one person he could entrust his life to.'

'How did you get to use Ada's phone?' Abel asked immediately, aware that she was one of Soni's lovers and wondering whether Ada knew about the different women his brother consorted with.

'She came here to see me. She needed to see whether I could help her get some money from the account, but you are the next of kin. And she wouldn't call you. She said you didn't like her. Anyway, I got your number once from Soni when I went on a trip to Asaba and he wanted us to meet, but I knew that if I sent the text from my phone you would think it was a scam, so when she left to use the restroom, I sent the message through her phone.'

'What time was this?'

'Must have been in the afternoon … About 3pm.'

'I didn't receive the text until dawn the next morning,' Abel told her.

'Network problems, I guess. I had to go on vacation soon after and I only returned two days ago.'

'Welcome back,' he said with a smile. She nodded with a flash of beautiful teeth. 'So, what's the issue with the account?'

'Nothing really. I just wanted us to meet and to say that if you need to access the account it can be done. I have spoken to our regional director.'

'That's good to know. We had issues with one of the banks but we finally got through. I wish you had been in town then.'

'Sorry about that. I had to go on vacation.'

'I understand. You and Soni were close, right? He seemed to have told you so many things.'

'We were good friends, yes. And he adored you. Spoke about you all the time as if you were some big man somewhere. I could never believe you were just a teacher.'

'Lecturer,' Abel said, and they both laughed.

'Well, if you need a friend to talk to or someone to hang out with, give me a buzz. I know nice places.' She rose.

Abel took the cue and rose too. 'It's been a pleasure,' He took her soft, slim fingers in his palm.

'Same here,' she said and Abel felt himself stir.

'Maybe we could hang out sometime,' he said, holding on to her hand and pushing the window a little wider.

'Sure. My weekends are pretty free.'

At the door, as Abel stepped out, he heard her say, 'One moment, please.'

'Yes?'

What she said next stunned him.

'I know this may sound callous and unfeeling but Soni promised me a new car for my birthday and it's next week Tuesday. I know he is still missing but I really need a new car and it's not as if he is broke. There is a lot of money in his account.'

Abel stood by the door and looked at her. In that moment, all artifices of sophistication were stripped away and what stood out were her fangs and claws. This was a Lagos Big Girl.

—

'Who is that woman?' Abel asked Santos as they walked to the car.

'Bros, she is Sabato's account officer,' Santos said and something in his voice made Abel stop mid-stride.

'Did she tell you about the car?' Abel asked in Igbo, and Santos sighed in defeat. 'Is that why you brought me here?'

'Yes. She told me Sabato promised her a car.'

'And how much did she promise you?'

'Two hundred K.'

'Santos, my brother is missing and you think I want to sleep with that shark so she can have a new car?'

'No vex, bros,' he said completely mortified. 'We gave that manager almost six million for helping. I thought we could get rid of him and use Sista Nicole.'

Sister Nicole! Abel opened his mouth to say something, then thought better of it. He was getting into the car when he heard someone shouting his name.

'Chiedu! Chiedu Dike!'

He looked up. A beefy mass of a man was puffing his way towards them.

'Nnamdi Nwankwo,' Abel cried as they hugged.

'I thought you were dead,' Nnamdi teased.

'I thought you were in prison?' Abel shot right back, and they both laughed. 'O boy, how many years now?'

'Six, maybe seven. I missed Sabato's wedding. You look good.' He took in Abel's clothes and shoes, all taken from Soni's wardrobe. 'Are you in Lagos now?'

'No. I came to spend time with my brother's family. Haven't you heard?'

'Heard what?'

'Soni is missing.'

'Missing? No. What happened?'

Abel wasn't sure whether Nnamdi was faking it, but he told him the story anyway.

'God forbid. I didn't hear. What's the police doing?'

'Still searching.'

'Na wa. Well, you must come and know my place. We should hang out; let me show you Lagos. You drink beer now, abi?' Nnamdi laughed. 'You were so fragile in those days. We used to bet you would die before we finished secondary school.' He laughed some more.

'God will punish all of you,' Abel said, laughing too.

'Ah, but you didn't die, so we lost our bets.'

They exchanged numbers with a promise to hang out.

Inside the car, an excited Santos was all teeth. 'Bros, that's Double N. Lagos Big Boy with a capital B.'

Abel ignored him.

'Drive to Alausa, governor's office.'

Stung by the snub, Santos started the car. As he hit the road he turned to Abel and said, 'I don't know Ikeja very well,'

Abel told him to drive down to Allen Avenue. They drove the length of Toyin Street, past the high-priced fashion boutiques and rows of new generation banks. Santos made a left at the roundabout and headed down Allen.

Abel – who had sent a text to Calista to ask for directions – looked out of the window and remembered the first time he came to Allen Avenue. The place had looked like the most impressive place on earth, especially that night, with the neon lights all ablaze.

It was the high street of the mainland with the most impressive array of shops, banks and finance houses. That was in the early to mid-nineties, before the collapse of the finance houses. Abel remembered how breathtaking it had been, then, for him to gaze upon the Oshopey Plaza at night in all its dazzling glory.

By the time they hit the Allen roundabout, Calista's text had come in, giving them precise directions. Abel remembered that going straight would lead to Adeniyi Jones while a 180-degree turn to the left would lead them back to the Ikeja under-bridge through Awolowo Road where the Ikeja Airport Hotel was. He remembered buying second-hand books under that bridge.

They drove about two kilometres down, past the right turn that led to Oregun and the traffic lights that ensured there was sanity for those coming towards Allen roundabout from Agidingbi and Oregun. Abel was happy to see that there were street signs everywhere telling you what street you were on or driving into. Years back, when he spent his first extended period in Lagos, there were no street signs and people would give you directions by saying, 'Drive into the street, turn left; you will see a water tank painted yellow. My house is second on your left.' God help you if someone moved the water tank or changed the colour.

Once they drove past the next roundabout at Agidingbi junction, Abel asked Santos to make a right. They drove down the road, then made a quick left. One more turn right and a left and they were flagged down at the gate. Abel identified himself and whom they had come to see.

'Hold on, sah,' the policeman said as he picked up the handset.

'Mr Haybel Dike,' he said mutilating Abel's name. Calista must have said something because he laughed and said, 'Madam, all na di same. Na omo ibo. Oya, go in sah,' he said waving them on to the car park.

Abel left Santos at the car. Calista was waiting outside the entrance.

'Did you come alone?' she asked hugging him.

'My cousin drove.'

'He can leave. I will drop you off at home. I am leaving early today. Did I tell you I resigned?'

'No. Why? I thought you came back for this?'

'Yes, but I am going for my postdoc at the Harvard School of Public Policy.'

'For how long?'

'Two years.' She led him inside, taking his handset and keys and dropping them in the tray before they passed through the metal detector.

There was a mobile police officer manning the entrance. She was dressed in a well-starched uniform that made her look like she had just stepped off the set of some dystopian movie.

'You look very sharp, my sister,' Abel complimented her.

'Be careful or I will cut you,' she replied and laughed.

'When do you leave?' Abel asked as Calista led him down a corridor to an office marked 'SSA Public Policy'.

'Next week.'

'That's cruel. I find you after ten years only to lose you again.'

'Wrong timing, Mr Dike.' She smiled. 'Come to America. Come with me.'

'Here you go again, always wanting to take me out of Nigeria.'

'And you don't want to leave Nigeria?'

'What for? The country needs me.' He laughed.

'Give me two minutes, OK. We will go see the CSO before lunch and then you can do with me as you please.' She threw her arms wide open, shaking her tits in his face.

'Your thoughts towards me are not good, Miss Adeyemi,' he said and kissed her.

While she cleared up, Abel sent a BB message asking Santos to drop the car off at home and close for the day.

The CSO was a tall, mild-mannered fellow with a slight stutter. He asked Abel a few questions, then put a call through to the commissioner of police, who directed Abel to a DCP at Panti.

'I will text him your number and he will call you, personally,' the commissioner told him. 'Let's see how we can help.'

Abel said his thanks and handed the phone back to the CSO.

They drove out to Pearl Garden Chinese restaurant on Isaac John. After lunch, Calista said she was tired so Abel drove. Heading out down Isaac John they made a right, drove past the Country Club and on to Mobolaji Bank Anthony, past the Sheraton on the left and the Ikeja cantonment on the right. Maryland looked tight, so Abel made a right turn and took the shortcut that wound its way beside the cantonment.

The long stretch that led from Mobolaji Bank Anthony into Ikorodu Road was called Onigbongbo, originally home to the Aworis and distinguished mostly by the fact that almost every house had a tomb outside. The residents buried their dead at home.

'How come you know these roads, eh, our man from Asaba?' Calista asked.

'Long story. I had this friend who used to live with Pa Okunzua, just around this corner,' Abel told her pointing around a bend. 'You know Pa Okonzua?' She nodded.

'Everyone knew Pa Okonzua with his funny predictions.' They both laughed.

'Well, I came here a few times to visit my friend.'

'What was his house like?' Calista asked as they entered Ikorodu road and made a right.

'Spooky, kind of, with lots of books. He used to just sit there with his glasses perched atop his nose and read newspapers or big fat books.'

Pa Okunzua was a self-styled psychic who seemed to have had a knack for making wrong predictions, especially about public figures.

Once, just before the 1979 elections, he predicted that the name of the winner was in the Bible. The nation had interpreted it to mean that it would either be Nnamdi Azikiwe, leader of the Nigeria People's Party, whose name was Benjamin, or Obafemi Awolowo, leader of the Unity Party of Nigeria whose name was Jeremiah.

Alas, Shehu Shagari – a Muslim candidate – won. Faced with a nation amused at his antics, Pa Okunzua quickly reached for the Bible and pointed to Judges 3:31, stating that Shamgar was the same as Shagari.

Ikorodu Road was free, but as they made it onto Town Planning Way at Ilupeju to connect with the Gbagada expressway en route to the Third Mainland Bridge, a group of policemen flagged them down.

'Oga, your driver's licence,' the policeman demanded when Abel wound down the window.

'Sorry, it's not with me in this car.' He had left his wallet in the car they drove out with.

'Park well and come down,' the officer barked, reaching for the AK-47 that hung from his shoulder.

'What's going on?' Calista asked, rousing herself. She had nodded off.

'Driver's licence, wahala.'

'Don't worry, I will handle it,' she said stepping out of the car.

'Madam, stay in the car,' the officer barked. 'I asked him to come down not you.'

'I want to speak to your superior officer.'

'He doesn't want to speak to you.' He stood in front of Calista, blocking her path.

'I want to speak to your superior officer,' she repeated, but he shoved her back so hard she slipped and fell.

Abel opened the door to help but another policeman hit him on the shoulder with the butt of his gun.

'Stay inside the car,' he barked.

Recoiling with pain, Abel stepped back inside the car.

'I tell you before; stay in the car,' the policeman barked, prodding Calista, who was back on her feet, with the barrel of his gun.

Cars had parked and a crowd had gathered. Calista stepped back into the car and picked up her phone. Abel heard her begin to speak as he was pulled out of the car and handcuffed. They pushed him to their patrol vehicle, which was parked right in front of a bank and asked him to step inside.

They let Abel sit there in handcuffs for close to five minutes while they went back to the road to harass other drivers. He marvelled at how easily things shifted in Lagos, how easily it was to cross the fault lines. One minute they were cruising along in an air-conditioned SUV and the next he was sitting at the back of a smelly patrol vehicle.

An officer was seated in the front passenger seat. He had a newspaper spread out in front of him but Abel could tell that he knew what was going on.

'What's wrong with your woman?' the policeman who had pushed Calista down asked as he sauntered up to Abel. 'Once they go to school abroad they won't have respect for men again.' He paused and Abel sensed that he wanted him to say something. When Abel didn't speak he gazed out at Calista, who was working the phone frantically, and said, 'It is men like you who are the ones spoiling them.'

The officer called out and the policeman went up to him. They conversed in low tones and then the policeman walked back to Abel.

'Driving without a licence and resisting arrest are serious offences. Wetin you wan do?' he asked, switching to pidgin, in negotiation mode.

'Wetin you want?' Abel asked, playing along.

He knew Calista would have contacted the CSO and commissioner of police. Help was on its way.

'Forty thousand and we can forget everything.' The policeman looked away. 'Person wey dey waka with Americanah must get money or e no go dey break the laws of Nigeria.'

'You still want money after putting me in handcuffs?' Abel asked. 'No, let's go to the station.'

The policeman clearly didn't expect that. He gazed at Abel for a while as if he was seeing him for the first time, then he hissed and went back to the officer. They conversed again before the policeman came back to Abel.

'You want to play hardball,' he said in a fake American accent. 'Co'pl, let's drive this bagger to the station.'

And that was when it all changed.

Tyres screeched, and six heavily armed, neatly dressed policemen jumped out of their van with guns drawn.

'Drop your weapons,' their leader barked. One of the policemen, the one at the farthest end, dropped his weapon and ran.

Abel was laughing hard by the time they uncuffed him and bundled the four policemen and their superior officer into the back of their patrol van.

'I am so sorry madam,' the officer apologised to Calista. 'They were on illegal duty. They had no right to be here and they will be dealt with. The commissioner sends his apologies.'

'He already called,' Calista said and spat straight in the face of the policeman who had pushed her down.

—

Abel didn't want them to incur unnecessary demurrage while Matthew Chu was away, so he agreed to go to his strip joint and sign the papers.

But it wasn't just about the papers. Abel was curious. He had seen strippers and strip joints in movies but he had never been to one. He was curious to see what it looked like up close.

So, at about 10pm, dressed and ready, he walked downstairs to find Santos. He wasn't in the living room where he had left him about an hour earlier.

'E dey sleep for guest room,' the house help told him.

Santos was sprawled on the bed in the guest room, the black pillowcase stained with drool, his red-booted feet dangling over the edge of the bed. Abel prodded him awake with a foot. He waited while Santos rinsed his mouth and washed his face.

When he went to get the car, Abel told Philo to change the sheets and pillowcases.

Driving in Lagos at night revealed it to be a small city with a distended belly. You could drive from Lekki to the airport in less than thirty minutes if you had a voracious appetite for speed, but in the daytime, Lagos was sluggish like a python that had swallowed something huge.

The traffic was the *something huge* clogging the gut of the city. The roads were bad and the arteries few, so once one was clogged the others would be too, causing a gridlock.

The roads were free that night but the streets were active. Coming into Ikeja from Mobolaji Bank Anthony, Santos drove into Opebi through the road that turned right beside the Sheraton Hotel. There were cars parked everywhere and if you wound down and listened you could hear fast-paced music pulsating. It was a Friday and people were actively seeking fun.

Gently swaying men and women hung around in clusters, talking or making out, feverish hands riding up short skirts. Lagos nights could be like that, shrouded under a haze of bacchanalia.

Allen was more animated, more in the moment.

'All these girls na ashewo,' Santos said as they drove past the Allen roundabout. 'Give dem hundred naira, dem go give you good time.'

Abel stole a quick look at him and wondered what Santos defined as 'good time'.

They made a right turn into Ogundana Street and then drove some two hundred metres before Santos finally found a stop as a Range Rover pulled out. There were luxury cars parked on both sides of the road, stretching all the way to the end. Business was good for Matthew Chu.

As they walked down to the club, Santos asked Abel whether he should call Matthew.

'He will give us VIP treatment,' he said, reaching for his phone, but Abel had told him not to. He wanted to experience the club as a normal punter without being chaperoned.

There were two bouncers at the entrance and a mobile policeman holding an AK-47 as casually as an artist would hold a brush while contemplating a new painting. He had the bored look of a man who provided a service no one really needed.

When they got to the head of the queue, they were asked to pay a two thousand naira entry fee, were patted down and had the back of their hands stamped with invisible ink. Stuck to the door was a loud sign – NO ENTRY IF YOU ARE NOT OF LEGAL AGE – but no one was there to check.

Inside, the music was loud and the air thick with cigarette smoke.

The joint was small and L-shaped. The stage stood in the right-angled crook of the L, allowing patrons on both ends to get a good view. It was a small rectangular space with a raised floor, about two feet off the ground, that held Abel's attention. It had two poles set about four feet apart and two naked girls shimmied on stage, each baring her sex as she slid down. They didn't seem very good at it, if what he saw in the movies was the standard.

Abel and Santos found a seat. There was an unrelenting air of desperation about the place. Abel had come expecting to see naked women dancing and grinding, but this was excessive and a tad depressing. He had never seen as many naked women all at once in one place, and even though he liked naked women, the nude conurbation had the unintended consequence of leaving him unaroused. There was a pall around the place, a strange displacement, and the low lighting that seemed to cast a deathly glow did not help.

He had come expecting nudity but this was a meat shop, a surfeit that left him nauseous.

A girl in a red top came up to them and asked what they wanted to drink. They ordered stout. She hadn't even stepped away when two girls with jiggling breasts planted themselves in front of Abel and Santos.

'Make I dance for you?' the taller of the two said, planting long fingers painted in different colours on Abel's crotch.

He smiled. 'Come back later.'

She did not return his smile as she walked away, wriggling her G-stringed ass. Santos had no qualms and as Abel turned, the other girl was already dancing, rubbing her ample backside against Santos' distended crotch.

He looked around. There were doors leading off the floors and most of them had what appeared to be stickers but on closer examination were actually instructions to patrons.

A FEE OF N4,000 IS CHARGED FOR RELAXING
WITH A GIRL IN VIP LOUNGE.

RESPECT YOURSELF NO CAMERA

Television screens showing pornographic movies hung from the corners like demented bats with flickering eyes. No one seemed to be watching, so Abel put it down to a need to create atmosphere, as if anybody walking in would mistake the place for a church.

The patrons were a mixed bunch. There were elderly men with beer bellies leering at the naked girls and sticking fingers into their dripping wetness. Quite a few of the men seemed bored, as if they would rather be somewhere else.

The professional types and younger boys were more eager. Most of the younger boys, those in their twenties, had girls with them and Abel wondered how a man convinces his date to come with him to a strip club.

The seats seemed like church pews: straight-backed benches with desks in front. The girls would lie on the desktops, spread their legs wide, place both legs on the patron's shoulders and sometimes grind themselves into a willing face. It was a bit too much for Abel but many of the men didn't seem to mind, nor did the girls, who didn't show any qualms about having fingers stuck inside them or having their breasts kneaded.

He saw a girl walk by and thought she looked like a student of his. Reaching out, he touched her hand. She turned to look at him. There was the briefest flicker of what looked like recognition, then her face clouded over and she sashayed away.

Abel sipped his drink, casting a quick look at Santos who was fondling the girl's breast, and then he let the music wash over him. They were playing Nigerian music. Davido. Olamide. Wande Coal. P-Square. IllBliss. Some he recognised and some he did not, but the music was loud and he let his mind drift with the sounds.

'Leave me,' he heard, and turned.

A girl was up and trying to get past her boyfriend and a stripper who was draped all over him like a second skin.

'I am going jor,' she said, pushing past them and running outside. The boy pushed the stripper away as he got up and chased after her, the bulge in his trousers making him walk funny.

'Oya, go and look for Matthew,' Abel said nudging Santos.

Santos pushed the girl aside, fished out two notes for her, then stood and adjusted his erection.

'Haba, I did not know you were here,' Matthew said, smiling expansively when Santos returned with him. 'I have been waiting for you in the VIP lounge. Abeg come,' he said leading Abel to a door.

He was the tallest Chinese man Abel had ever seen. He had a full beard and walked with a Nigerian swagger, arms thrust out as if he owned the universe.

He pushed the door open and let them upstairs.

'How long have you been in Nigeria?' Abel asked as Matthew preceded them into his office and indicated the seats.

'Long time. Na we show Chinese people the way,' he said in pidgin and laughed. 'When I come to Lagos, the only Chinese they know is Bruce Lee and Bruce Lee is American sef. But I like Lagos. In this town anything can happen. Very good things and very bad things, no be so?'

He pulled out a folder, spread out the papers in front of Abel and produced a pen from his pocket. 'Sign here, here and here,' he said, pointing, but Abel indicated that he wanted to read. 'Ah, a cautious man. You read before you sign; good.' Matthew fetched a bottle of Hennessy from a cupboard. He placed the bottle on the table, produced three plastic cups and poured drinks. He and Santos made small talk while Abel read. He asked Santos whether they needed girls for the night and Santos nodded towards Abel and shook his head.

'Oh, your broda doesn't do that, eh? You don't tell him our girls are clean? Sweet, clean pussy,' Matthew said, more to Abel than to Santos.

Abel looked up, smiled and continued reading.

Done. He signed and downed his drink.

'Santos knows your people, so I will put this in his hands. Is that OK?' Abel asked.

Matthew nodded. 'Very OK. They all sabi Santos anyway.'

'We need to go now.' Abel extended a hand.

'Ahh, we have clean girls here. You don't want some ficki-ficki? I bring you the cleanest girls,' Matthew offered again as they shook hands.

Abel thanked him and said he was good, then led the way downstairs and out to the car.

—

They drove home in silence, Abel studiously avoiding talking to Santos. He was still miffed by the encounter with Dr Nicole at the bank and Santos' part in the charade.

Once he got home, Abel stripped and stepped under the shower. He knew it was all in his head, but it felt as if the strip joint had left a layer of dirt on his skin and he needed to scrub it off.

Santos launched into another apology the next morning the moment Abel sat down beside him to plan their itinerary, but Abel had asked him to shut it.

'How much do you earn?' Abel asked.

'Eighty thousand naira, bros.'

'Eighty thousand naira.' The idiot earned more money than him. He made a mental note to speak to Ada and the accountant about increasing Santos' salary before he sold them all to the devil in his quest for money. Abel could well understand how it must feel for Santos to sit so close, to smell and taste wealth all day and yet remain acutely aware that none of it was his. He had heard many stories of how people like Santos, feeling resentment, would commit all sorts of atrocities against their benefactor. Their excuse was always simple and the same: it was all a hustle.

They had a date at Panti to meet the deputy commissioner of police, who was now in charge of Soni's case. Whether criminal or not, Panti was known to everyone. It was called Panti after the street on which it was located. When a criminal said his case had been transferred to Panti, people raised their hands to their heads and got all bug-eyed with fear.

The official name was the State Criminal Investigations Department (SCID) and the belief was that any case that did not get cracked by the team of detectives at Panti would never be solved. People also believed that any criminal who was not broken at Panti must be the devil himself.

The deputy commissioner of police assigned to Soni's case had called Abel the previous evening, just as the commissioner had said he would, a few minutes after Calista dropped him off at home. The incident with the policemen at Ilupeju had soured everything and their plans to spend time together didn't happen after all.

'Why didn't she come in?' Ada asked when Abel came outside to meet her by the pool. She had a guest and they were watching a Nigerian movie.

'Who?'

'Your female friend. I saw her drop you off.'

'She had to go someplace.' He nodded to acknowledge the lady's greeting.

'She is a pretty one.' Ada winked.

'Not as pretty as you,' Abel said and flopped into a chair.

He saw the woman smile at Ada and open her palms quizzically as if to say *What's going on here?*

'Don't mind Ada, she likes to tease,' Abel said to the woman in response to her unuttered question.

'Oh, I am the tease now,' Ada said. 'You were the one who called me hairy, eh, remember?'

'You don't forget things?' Abel asked with mock seriousness. 'What are you girls watching?'

'*Two Brides and a Baby*,' her friend answered.

'Who is in it?'

'When did you start liking Nollywood flicks?' Ada asked. 'Or is it my friend you like?'

'Ada!' her friend cried and they both giggled.

'All of the above,' Abel said and rose.

———

DCP Bola Balogun was a tall, slim, slightly stooping man with a deep voice. He welcomed Abel into his little office, which had been done up in red hues from the rug to the upholstered chairs.

'When the commissioner starts calling us about cases it looks as if we are not doing our jobs,' he began and there was no mistaking the note of displeasure in his voice.

'Oga, that's not what happened. I did not go to make a report. I was at the government house and ran into the CSO. Somehow my brother's issue came up and he promised to assist.' Abel quickly filled him in on what the situation was like.

'Your brother's case is a difficult one to crack,' he said, as if he hadn't heard Abel. 'It appears he was abducted and we believe the abductors must have been riding with him in the car. There must have been a struggle, which was why the car was found in the ditch. What happened afterwards is anyone's guess because they didn't ask for a ransom and we haven't found a body. Whoever did this wanted your brother fixed for good. If we had a ransom demand then we would have a lead to pursue, but as things stand, it's as if your brother simply disappeared from the face of the earth.'

He pressed a bell on his table and a dark, burly policeman stepped in.

'Kunle, get me DSP Umannah.' A minute later he introduced the man. 'DSP Umannah, please meet Mr Dike.' Abel and the officer shook hands. 'The commissioner asked me to transfer his brother's case from Ofio to you with immediate effect. Ofio has handed you the files, right?'

'Yes, sir.'

'Good. The commissioner wants quick answers. I need quicker answers. The family is anxious. You have five weeks. Gentlemen.' He rose.

Abel took the hand he extended, said his thanks and followed Umannah out. Umannah's office was tiny and stacked with papers. He seemed like the brainy kind. He settled down behind a desk and motioned for Abel to sit in one of the chairs opposite him.

'This place is hot and there is no light,' he said, pushing the window open.

'But there was light now at the DCP's office,' Abel said

'That is the dividend of being the boss,' Umannah said and laughed. 'You remember George Orwell's book, *Animal Farm*?'

'Yes, I do,' he said.

'"Some animals are more equal than others",' Umannah quoted and laughed. Abel laughed too, liking him. He was light-skinned the way people from his Cross River area could be and he spoke with the slightest hint of an accent, the type people called 'Calabar accent'.

'See, I will put my all into this because I knew your brother and he helped me once.'

'You knew him?'

'Yes. I was at Area F when he was detained there. I was a much younger officer then.'

'Really. That was like seven years ago or so. I came to bail him out but I am not sure I met you. I remember some woman at the counter stole his ring.'

'Service charge, you mean,' he said and laughed. Abel laughed too.

'Well, while in detention, I helped him buy food, water and stuff. I was even the one who sent word to his brother in Asaba.'

'I am the brother.'

'Wow. He was scared of how you would react but he said you were the only person he could trust. I thought you would be older.'

'I am older.'

'I know; I meant older as in older. Anyway, he kept in touch after he was released and a few years back, when my son needed surgery for a hernia, he paid the hospital bill. He was a nice guy.'

'Thank you,' Abel said. The more he heard stories of how his brother revered him the more he wondered why he had never noticed. It felt sometimes as if they were talking about two different people, not his brother and him.

'I will put my best men on this right away. I read Inspector Ofio's report and I already have a theory, but give me a week or two and I should have something conclusive for you and the family.'

Abel thanked him and stood to go, but Umannah's voice stopped him at the door.

'Abel, this is high stakes. I don't want to raise your hopes too much but I will help you find the missing pieces so that all of this can make better sense.'

'Thank you so very much,' Abel said and walked out.

—

Calista was home so he had Santos drop him off there.

She had her bathrobe on when she opened the door and as soon as Abel stepped into the living room, he tugged at the sash and the robe came undone. She was naked underneath. Abel sank to his knees and buried his face between her legs, inhaling her deeply.

'Have you eaten?' she asked, stroking his head like a mother would a wayward child.

'This will do for now,' he said as he lifted her and carried her upstairs.

Abel drifted off to sleep after their lovemaking and by the time he woke up Calista had made lunch and laid the table.

They ate and returned to bed. 'Hold me,' Abel said. She held him and once again he was a twenty-two-year old who had just received word that his father was dead. Soni had gone drinking once the news was broken to them and would be carried back to the room hours later, totally drunk.

Abel, on the other hand, had found Calista and snuggled up to her, crying and talking, pouring out his fears, his angst and his innermost thoughts.

That was almost fourteen years ago but now he was back in that place and Calista was there with a thirsty ear to lap up his stream of words. He started with the text message and explained how, for so many years since the day he came to bail Soni out of Area F, he had dreaded receiving a call that intimated something terrible.

'That was why, every time he offered me something, I declined. But he always insisted. You know, money, a car, stuff. I felt that by saying no, I was expressing my disapproval and hoping that things would turn out differently.'

He told her about the woman and the girl at the bank, how the girl had torn off her clothes, stripping herself naked in full view of everyone to get away from the stink. He told Calista that that was how he felt at times, living in Soni's house, spending his money, luxuriating in the opulence that had been made possible by crime, like he was wallowing in something dirty, and being tainted by the stink of it all.

He told her about the meeting with DCP Balogun and how he had sensed that maybe the police already knew more than they were telling.

'He said, "Whoever did this wanted your brother fixed for good." There was something ominous about those words. Something very final.'

'Abel, whoever did this meant it. That's what I think he was trying to say,' Calista told him, teasing his left nipple with the tip of her tongue. Abel laughed and pushed her gently away.

He told her about Ada and his disturbing feelings towards her.

'I don't know how much longer we can keep away from each other. If we open that door, everything will break down,' he said, rising from the bed and pacing.

'So what are you going to do about your feelings for her?' Calista asked sitting up, lotus style on the bed, her sex exposed to him.

Leaning against the wall, away from the bed, and contemplating her question, Abel watched her sitting there, her naked pubis fringed by the light fluff that tapered into the parted folds of her labia. He regarded her with a cocked brow, suddenly lightheaded from a surfeit of desire. She seemed to him like a deep well from which he would never be able to drink enough, but there was, above all, in that pose, a quality that made her look like a goddess; his petite Buddha of desire.

Abel pushed her back on the bed and mounted her like an eager steed and this time there was not just need but an insatiable hunger. A lifetime or two later, sweating and panting, Abel held her close from behind, his flaccid member dripping spunk onto her bed sheet like a one-eyed slug.

'I wish you weren't leaving so soon; maybe I would have moved in here,' he told her.

'Rent a place,' she said turning to face him, her breasts heaving. 'You can afford it.'

Abel thought about it for a while then shook his head. 'It won't look good. What will I tell her, my auntie, people? All that big house and I have to go and rent a place. It would even seem as if I am already staking a claim on his money. No.'

'Then it will happen someday. It would be easier if he were dead. In Africa, men have always married their brothers' wives. But if he is not dead and he returns, there would be issues.'

'I want him to return,' Abel said, a wistful look on his face. He told her about how everyone he met told him how much

Soni spoke about him, how much, it now appeared, his brother adored him.

'I never knew. It feels as if I didn't even know who he was. I would treat him a lot better if he came back.'

'I always knew he liked you and respected you even though he tried to mask it with bravado,' Calista said, pulling Abel on top of her. 'I remember how he used to call me 'The Coloniser of Abel.' She nibbled his left ear, her warm breath fanning his neck.

'Once, at a party, he had been drinking, and he came up to me and said, "Your pussy must be gold-plated, the way Abel is stuck to you." We can't all be dogs, I told him and he laughed that his big laugh and said, "We can't all be saints, you mean. My brother gives everyone a bad conscience. He has always been the good son. I can never be like him. Everything good comes to him. Come, let us dance." And he pulled me to the dance floor.'

'Where was I?'

'You were there, looking bored. I could never figure it out, why you couldn't stand parties.'

'Too many people, Calista. I have always liked to be alone.' He told her about his job as a lecturer in Asaba where he taught English literature. 'I always wanted to be a teacher. But right now, I am not even sure what I have become.'

'You have become hard.' She reached between his legs.

'This woman; you will kill someone.' He tickled her and sired happy giggles.

—

The house was in darkness when he got home. There was an outage and the generator wouldn't come on. Ada was outside at the shed with Philo and the gateman was busy poking inside the generator.

'When was it serviced last?' Abel asked.

'I can't remember. Soni handles all these things,' she said, a sob catching in her throat.

'Let me see.' Abel took the torch from the gateman. He checked the oil gauge; it was low. He knew some generators wouldn't come on if there was no oil. 'Is there engine oil in the house?'

Ada wasn't sure so he asked the gateman to go buy a gallon. While he was gone, Abel took out the spark plugs and cleaned them.

With oil in the generator and the spark plugs cleaned he tried again. The generator rattled for a bit, caught and roared into life.

'Thanks,' Ada said touching him lightly on the shoulder.

Inside, he took off his clothes, ran a bath, dropped a tablet of deliciously scented bath salts he found in Soni's drawer and stepped in. He lay back in the tub and contemplated whether to turn on the whirlpool. He reached behind and switched it on. He needed to relax.

He picked up the book he had left on the chair in the bathroom and tried to read, but somehow Sula's story didn't interest him. So, he shut his eyes and tried to blank out his thoughts. He wanted to switch off, forget where he was, try not to remember that his brother was missing; just soak and forget.

'Are you OK? Abel?'

Ada was sitting on the stool in the bathroom and staring at him.

'I knocked and knocked and when you didn't answer I came into the room. When I didn't see you I came in here. Are you OK?' she asked again.

He realised that he had dozed off.

'Yes. I just needed to soak and relax,' he said, placing his hands over his crotch even though he knew she couldn't see that far.

'I need more than that now. I think I am going crazy.'

'What happened?'

'Everything. But this night when the generator didn't come on, I just lost it. What do I know about a generator? Soni always took care of all that. Imagine if you weren't here. This is beginning to get to me. What did the police say today?'

'I met with the DCP. I am not so sure he was happy to have received a call from the commissioner. But he has reassigned the case to a more senior and experienced officer. I like the new guy. He knew Soni too.'

'Everyone knew Soni,' she said but her mind was far away. 'See, I don't know how to say this but you know, your brother was involved with so many women, some of them married. You know that?'

'Ada, what is this about?'

'I have been thinking, you know, a jealous husband, boyfriend. I can imagine what he would do if he found me with another man. If this was about a woman, I would hate him. I always told him, don't bring an STD into this house and don't let one of your women embarrass me. That was all I asked for.'

'I don't think this is about a woman,' Abel said reaching for the towel. 'Could you turn around for a second?'

He stepped out of the tub, pushed the knob to drain the water, and towelled himself dry before he joined Ada, who was sprawled on the couch in his room.

'We used to make love here all the time,' she said running her palm over the soft fabric of the couch. 'Soni never liked making love on the bed. He said it wasn't good for his nine inches.'

Abel pulled on a pair of boxers and a T-shirt. He sat on the bed, placed a pillow between his legs to hide his rising erection, and settled down to listen. He could sense an urge in her to talk and unburden herself.

'I am sure we conceived Zeal in the car or kitchen or the living room. Soni was always looking for the craziest spots.'

She paused and then sat up.

'Come sit beside me,' she told him but Abel shook his head. He had a huge erection already.

'Just talk, I want to listen.'

'You know, when Zeal was born, he wanted him to be named Abel,' she went on as if there had been no pause. 'Did he tell you that?'

He shook his head. 'No, he never did.'

'Well he did but I said no. I hated you then.' She laughed. 'I didn't want my son reminding me of you every time I called or heard his name.'

'Zeal is a lovely name,' Abel told her.

'Yes, it is.' She leaned back into the couch and fell silent. Abel regarded her for a while, wondering what crazy thoughts were raging in her head.

She was dressed in denim shorts and a fitted T-shirt that showed off her bosom. He watched her and was surprised to hear her snoring softly. She had fallen asleep. He waited a while, then went over to the couch and covered her with a duvet before climbing back into bed. When he woke up later that night, Ada was in his bed, her arms wrapped around him.

———

She was gone by the time he woke up the next morning and she made no mention of the previous night as they had breakfast together after dropping Zeal off at school. She was unusually quiet and he assumed that she was thinking about having spent the night curled up in his bed.

After breakfast, Abel watched CNN then went upstairs to read and listen to music. He didn't have anything planned for the day. He just wanted to laze and catch his breath.

Santos sauntered into his room a little after 10am.

'Bros wahala dey o,' he said as he came to sit beside Abel on the couch.

'Wetin happen?' Abel asked, suddenly apprehensive. Lagos had that effect on him. It was a city always looking for ways to upset one's plans, like a garden blooming with anxiety.

Placing a finger to his lips, Santos whispered even though they were alone.

'Today is Iyawo's birthday. I just remembered now.'

'Are you sure?'

He nodded. 'Yes. I saw it on her Facebook page and on her DP, see.' He handed Abel his Blackberry.

It really was Ada's birthday. Abel handed the phone back to him.

'Go and bring out the car. We need to buy her cake and a gift.'

He showered in a hurry and they drove out to Victoria Island. There was a cake shop behind the Zenith Bank branch on Ajose Adeogun, Santos told him, and they drove there. Abel bought a cake and then they drove to a gift shop on Sanusi Fafunwa where he picked up a birthday card.

'What kind of gift do you think she would like?' Abel asked.

'Iyawo likes bags and dresses,' he told Abel. 'And I sabi where Sabato dey buy clothes for her.'

It was to a nondescript shop, tucked in between two houses on Akin Adesola, almost adjacent to Adeola Odeku, that Santos led him. It was the kind of shop you would never walk into unless someone brought you. Its location was not susceptible to serendipity.

The owner was a dark, heavily built woman of indeterminate age. Her clothing and gait suggested youthfulness, but her face was creased with lines etched by the passage of time and something that seemed like trauma. Abel could not put his finger on it but he surmised from her forced gaiety a need to keep up appearances as well as a stratagem for fleecing you.

'Na my bros wife,' Santos began. 'Today is her birthday and Oga Sabato no dey. This is Sabato's big bros.'

She greeted Abel with a smile as wide as a saucer and asked what he wanted. He told her a bag and a gown would be fine.

'I have this lovely tan bag. A Burberry. It just arrived,' She pulled open a drawer.

Abel wasn't sure what she meant by tan. The bag was light brown but he took it from her. 'And the dress; I take it you know her size? Something black would be cool.'

'Ada is a size twelve and I have the perfect LBD for her.' She flicked through gowns on a rack and pulled out a black dress with a plunging neckline. It had a belt with a light brown – or what she called tan – cowry-shaped buckle.

'They will go together,' the shop owner said, smile in place and obviously pleased with herself. 'And Ada has the shoes to go with them.'

Abel almost screamed when she told him what the clothes cost.

'I don't have that much here but I will send Santos back to you with the balance. Is that OK?'

The woman looked from Abel to Santos then smiled and said, 'Sure; your brother and his wife are my big customers. I will expect Santos.'

She wrote him a receipt, packed their purchases and had one of her girls carry them to the car.

Abel couldn't shake off the total amount. For a dress and a bag, he had spent three months' salary.

'Bros, you have to buy her champagne. Sabato no dey miss am o.'

'I have run out of cash,' Abel said.

'I sabi one guy. We go collect then I go come back come square dem.'

Abel waited in the car while Santos fetched two bottles of Moët & Chandon Rosé Impérial.

'Na dis one madam and her friend like well well,' he told Abel.

Santos also had two bottles each of white and red wines.

By the time they got home, three of Ada's friends had arrived and Abel was happy when she shrieked and ran into his arms as Santos delivered the cake and card.

Inside the card, he had inscribed a small poem:

To Ada,
Wife and Mother
There shall be seasons of refreshing
When we snatch joy from the fierce grip of pain
In due season and more, we shall rejoice again
Suffused with trilling laughter and joy unspoken
Happy birthday, from Abel and Zeal.

'Beautiful poem,' Abel heard one of her friends say as he walked away.

'Ada is so lucky. I can't remember the last time a man wrote me a poem,' another said.

'Must have been in secondary school,' said a third, and they all burst into laughter.

—

They dined at Villa Medici.

Ada wore the black dress and it was beautiful. She inhabited it as if it had been made especially for her. Abel hadn't noticed but it didn't just have a plunging neckline; it also had a low back that slinked all the way down.

She looked beautiful in it and Abel was thrilled to see all eyes turn to them as they walked in. His brother had indeed 'gone to the market', as one of his aunts loved to say, 'with his eyes wide open'.

They shared a bottle of 1990 Chianti with their meal. The antipasti was toasted bread with tomato, olives, mozzarella, meat, and balsamic vinegar in olive oil, while the main course was pasta, baked tomato and lamb chops.

He had ordered the Chianti because he remembered that it was the drink of choice for Anthony Hopkins' character in *Silence of the Lambs* and he'd always wondered what kind of drink it was and what it would taste like. Now he knew. And there was something else he was conscious of now. He was moving slowly but surely out of the realm of 'what if' and 'how would it be'. These days, whatever he wished for that money could buy was instantly possible and imminently available. There were no what ifs. If he wanted it, he could have it.

He had toyed many times with thoughts of moving money from Soni's accounts into his. As things stood, everything was still in Soni's name and available to him since he was next of kin, but if Soni's body was found tomorrow, the balance would shift. Having died intestate, all he owned would revert to his widow. Where would that leave him? Penniless in his hovel in Asaba, and only if he still had a job to go back to. But every time the thought chanced upon him, Abel would push it aside because it seemed cheap, wicked and opportunistic. He was in Lagos to find his brother, he told himself. Not to amass wealth.

The house was quiet and in partial darkness when they got home. Philo had stayed up and Abel could see that she had been watching a Nollywood movie on Africa Magic while she waited.

'Come dance with me,' Ada said, preceding him up the stairs, and he had difficulty peeling his eyes from her behind.

'Tonight?' Abel asked.

'Yes, tonight. It's my birthday, old man.'

He had never been inside her room before. It was beautiful and done up in soft pink and lilac.

One wall was covered entirely with paintings; small frames that looked no bigger than 12 x 10s, and they were all nude portraits by an artist whose work seemed familiar but whose name he could not see in the dim light. Most of them were merely stylised images with lines and highlighted bits; others were full frontals with highly realised depictions of the breasts and pubic region.

'You like?' she asked with a smile as she kicked off her shoes and inserted a disk into the CD player. A strong male voice he didn't recognise filled the room.

'Who is this?' he asked as she fell into his arms.

'Al Jarreau,' she told him, her head on his shoulder. 'Wait for the magic.'

Abel could feel her warm breath on the nape of his neck and smell the whiff of the wine on it – delicious. He wanted to kiss her badly, ravenously, to peel the black dress off her body and make mad love to her. Instead he held her close, glad he could mask his erection, having traded his normal boxer shorts for new Y-fronts he had found in his brother's closet.

The song was on replay and after the third play, he told her he had to go to bed.

Abel had just finished brushing his teeth and was settling into bed when he heard her sobbing, thick wracking sobs that wafted over the pause in the music and broke his heart into a million tiny shards. He grabbed a pillow and covered his ears to keep out the sound.

—

There was a text message from DSP Umannah on his phone when he woke up the next morning.

We have made an arrest. Please come in as early as you can.

Abel must have thought about that text a hundred times before he got to Panti. He was both anxious and elated. Would the arrested person lead them to Soni? Would they find him alive or dead? What would he do when Soni returned home? Pack up and move to Asaba, or move into the room Soni had prepared for him and play Uncle to Zeal while his blood boiled for Ada? Had he journeyed so far from Asaba that he would never be able to retrace his steps? A million questions assailed his thoughts as he drove, his knuckles shiny as he held tight to the steering wheel. He didn't tell Ada about the text message and he had asked Santos to wait for him at home while he ran a quick errand.

'Bros, you wan go see your babe for 1004?' Santos asked with a wink. Abel scowled and asked him to wash the X5.

Umannah was drenched in sweat and he had blood on his sleeves when Abel got to the station.

'False alarm, false alarm,' he said and Abel thought he would fall.

His emotions were in conflict; disappointment and what seemed, to his horror, like relief. He wanted his brother to be found or did he not? Things were not so black and white any more. He was moving slowly but inexorably (he realised with a shock that seemed like a violent kick to the small of the back), into a grey world of doubts and thoughts that he did not think he could allow to bud into words. He was getting to a point where he was not sure he could easily recognise himself if he bumped into himself in a dark alley.

Abel flopped into the chair DSP Umannah offered him.

'He came to the bank to cash your brother's cheque. It was torn from one of the chequebooks Soni's wife and accountant told us was missing. We had asked the bank to flag the cheque number series, so when he presented it we were alerted. We brought him in four days ago. At first he refused to talk but then we encouraged him to,' Umannah said with a wink as he sat down.

'He confessed someone gave him the chequebooks. From the figures in the stubs, they assumed the owner would be rich so they found a way to check the account balance. What they found made them greedier, and with the help of a lady in the bank, they were able to forge his signature. Anyway, we made more arrests last night and that was when I was confident enough to alert you. But after working on them all night and this morning, we realised what happened. The third person was among the first to chance upon your brother's car. It was half inside the gutter. The cabin lights were on and music was playing. He said he thought the person was drunk and had fallen into the ditch. Of course, when he looked into the car and around the ditch he didn't find anyone. He waited for a while, thinking that the car owner may have gone to get help and would come back. After a short while, when he didn't see anyone, he looked inside the car again. That was when he saw the chequebook on the floor mat. He reached in and took it. The next day when he walked by and saw the car still there, he must have felt some remorse, so he called 911 and reported to the operator that a Jaguar was lying in the ditch.'

'Did he really make a call?' Abel asked

'We checked his call logs; he did. Anyway, we are keeping them for attempted fraud. You want to see them?'

Abel thought about it. 'Yes.'

The men looked like they had received serious 'encouragement' to talk. They had been beaten and two of them had black eyes.

It was the woman who made Abel freeze. She was tall and pretty, and even in her jeans and T-shirt she looked out of place in that dingy cell.

'That's the lady banker who assisted them,' Umannah said.

Abel's mouth was hanging open. It was Dr Nicole.

—

Tormented by his feelings and oppressed by the delinquency of his thoughts, Abel locked himself in the room the whole day, refusing to go outside. He berated himself as he wondered what had gone wrong. When had the sea change happened? When had he moved from brother-in-law to this thing he did not recognise?

Two short months ago he was happy enough to be a teacher, to exist in his little room in Asaba, go to school, read his novels, drink a stout or two and go to bed each night, alone or with a partner when the opportunity presented itself. He was happy to be well and alive and living the life he had wished for himself since he was a mere boy. But all that now seemed like some millennia ago. He had been sucked in, as if by sorcery, by Lagos and the quicksand of comfort and luxury and he was beginning to struggle to keep his head clear.

A friend had told him once: 'You know, living a life of luxury is one thing you don't need to be trained for.'

How true, he thought, as he lay in his brother's huge, luxurious bed, his mind filled with lust as he wondered whether Ada, who was singing and pottering about next door, was naked, half-naked or fully clothed.

She was constantly in his head, like the strains of a bad song that takes up residence in your brain and refuses to be exorcised. He had wet dreams and huge arousals just thinking about her and it surprised him because he was a man who generally preferred monogamy. Usually, with Calista satisfying his needs, he would not bother with another woman. But with Ada, it was different.

He continually tried to catch lewd glimpses: her breasts when she bent to pick up her son, her panties when, in a careless moment, she forgot to keep her legs together – something, always. Around her, Abel was, in many ways, like a teenager hungry for pleasures. He knew that if that door suddenly opened, the one that separated his room from hers, only God would save them.

It was made more difficult by the fact that he did not fully understand his sister in-law. He knew she felt something but it was difficult to decipher. One minute, she was lying in his bed; the next she was treating him like what he was – a not-well-liked brother-in-law. She was a woman adept at masking her feelings, allowing you to see only that which she felt you ought to see.

Occasionally, Abel caught a glimmer of the steel in her. He would hear it inflected in her voice when she spoke to a driver, the guard or even Philo. It was there in moments when, like all humans, she dropped her guard and lowered that mask he felt she wore so well.

She could play the grieving wife searching for her husband or the loving mother tending her young child. She could play the loving sister-in-law, especially when Auntie Ekwi was around, but something in her actions, her words, the way she took control of things and situations told him that she was not a woman to be trifled with.

Abel had always taken pride in his ability to read people, to see beneath the veneer of affability that sometimes masked nastiness, but with Ada he was unsure, even though he was clear in his mind, since he started living under the same roof as her, that she was a woman who you handled with caution. He knew that deep beneath the beauty and cultivated airs was a woman who would not forgive or forget or let go when she needed to sink her teeth into you and lock her jaw tight.

He was sure, for instance, that if the tables were turned and she had the purse strings, life would not be so easy for someone who, to paraphrase Marcus Aurelius, ate her bread but did not do her will. And he shivered at the thought that he would not be exempt.

Thinking about Ada also made him think about Soni. Who had sold him out? What had he done wrong? Was it about money, a woman, a careless word or a refusal to be cheated? Soni could be stubborn when he felt he was being had.

Abel wondered what thoughts were on his mind when he realised that he was riding with Judases who had played thirty shekels with his life. How had Soni been taken? At gunpoint, with a threat, a mean hand across his neck, pinning him to the seat, cutting off air, causing him to veer off the road? Had he cried? Did he call for him or for their mum? Did he struggle or had he tried to run? As a child Soni had been a good runner but athletics had been no more than a means for him to attract girls. Was he scared and did he go with his abductors knowing that it was over and that his sins had finally caught up with him?

If he was dead, how did it happen? Had he been tortured? Was it a drawn-out process intended to give the most pain? He thought of all the movies he watched and books he read where family members would be told of their recently departed: 'It was quick. There was, thankfully, no pain.' And he wondered, as he did all the time, did it matter? The person was dead anyway and whether quick or drawn out, did the dead care? Or were these things we told ourselves to ameliorate the pain, to dull the ache of loss?

If, as many people insisted, there was no heaven or hell, no afterlife, if this life ended the moment the last breath was drawn, what did it matter how one died – happy, sad or in torturous pain? He hid under the duvet, his thoughts burning holes in his brain, wishing, without conviction, that the darkness would eclipse all, hide him from the man he was becoming, one he was finding tough to come to terms with.

He remembered Dr Nicole at Panti and his consternation.

'Why?' he had asked her.

'Did you ever ask your brother why?' she fired back with a hiss.

Abel had staggered out, the blood pounding in his ears. What demons drove the people in Lagos to do the things they did? He had read, the previous weekend, about two brothers who killed their older brother and sold bits and pieces of his body parts to ritualists. Luck ran out on them when neighbours got worried about the smell and alerted the authorities.

After he left the station, Abel sat in the car for a few minutes to calm his nerves. In there, under the blazing noon sun, he shuddered and wondered whether that same demon was already taking possession of him too.

Sleep claimed him in the darkness under the duvet and he dreamt, transported to when they were kids. They were on their way home and it was threatening to rain, so Soni suggested taking a shortcut through an orchard.

'You can't pass through here,' three boys told them.

'Soni, let's go,' Abel called but Soni was adamant.

Every time he made to pass, the boys would block his path and push him back. Then Soni threw a punch and the next moment fists and legs were flying.

Abel froze, watching as the boys knocked his brother to the ground. It started to rain and Abel was shivering and screaming but the legs and fists kept pounding until Soni disappeared into the ground.

Abel woke with a start. Ada was in the room.

'I have been knocking,' she said, parting the blinds.

Abel pushed aside the duvet and got off the bed. He passed water in the bathroom and then returned to bed.

Ada, who had settled on the couch, got up and uncovered a dish she had brought in on a tray. It was his favourite meal – jollof rice and smoked fish.

'Eat, Mr Dike,' she teased. 'You need a beer, or will water do?' She tapped against the wall to reveal a refrigerator Abel hadn't realised was there.

'What else is hidden in these walls?' He stood to check out the wall-recessed refrigerator.

He shut it and tapped the wall, but it didn't open.

'You need to say the password,' Ada said, her eyes smiling.

'What's the password?'

'A-B-E-L.' She laughed. 'Just tap three times; it will swing open.'

Abel tapped three times and the door swung open.

'I never noticed.' He took a can of beer from the fridge.

'Some German guy fixed it up for Soni. He was very proud of it.' She sat down.

'It's quite impressive,' Abel said, still marvelling. He tucked into the rice. 'Have you eaten?'

'Yes, a little. When I cook, I lose my appetite.'

'Well, I didn't cook. I am freaking hungry.' The rice was good: tasty and piping hot. The kind of food that made you sweat by the second spoon. 'You cook very well.'

She took a mock bow. 'Daalu,' she said in Igbo. 'You like listening to the news but you never watch the TV in here.' She picked up the remote control.

'I know. Blame it on my father. He always said the bedroom was for rest. He never even listened to his radio in bed. I got it from him.'

'Hmm, Soni always tuned in to CNN once we woke up. But this TV was mostly for bad things. He has a stack of naughty movies at the back there.' She pointed. 'You like?'

'No. I would feel inadequate. I am not 9 inches.' They both laughed.

'Your brother, eh. You know I didn't know about the 9 inches thing for a long time except that we would be out somewhere and a guy or girl would pass by and hail him, "9 Inches, long time!", "9 Inches, what's up?" And they always gave me this look, you know, like I was the latest victim. So, finally I asked him and the idiot worked up an erection and then brought a ruler. See, he said.'

'Was it 9 inches long?' Abel asked.

'Of course, it wasn't. The foolish man had been cheating all the while. "The missing inch only appears inside the, you know," he told me and I wacked his pecker with the ruler. He was in pain for almost one week.'

Abel choked on his food from laughing so hard. 'I always knew he was making it up. Foolish boy.'

Abel's phone rang; it was Nnamdi calling to confirm whether they were still good for Friday night. Abel told him it was OK.

'You know Nnamdi?' Abel asked, and Ada nodded.

'The contractor guy?' she said.

'Contractor?' Abel asked. 'I thought he was a "guy man",' he said, using the codename for 419 scammers.

'He stopped; went clean years back. Then he hit this billion-naira deal with MTN or Airtel and became large.'

'Really ... He is grown very big too. He used to be a skinny boy.'

'I haven't seen him in a while. You know Soni never visited anyone even though we always had guests. But I see him in the papers and stuff.'

When Ada took the dishes out, Abel undressed and got in the shower.

He walked out naked to find Ada sitting there, leafing through a magazine.

'Wow, cover yourself,' she told him without lowering her gaze. 'That's almost 3 inches,' she laughed.

Abel pulled on his discarded boxers, shaking his head, and settled in the bed. 'You are something else, you know.'

'I try. Let's go see a movie. I need to breathe before I get cabin fever cooped up in this house.'

They saw a Nigerian movie, *Tango with Me*, produced and directed by Mahmood Ali-Balogun and argued about the ending on their way to Bar Beach, where Ada said they should spend the rest of the evening before going home.

'What kind of ending is that?' Abel asked. 'No Nigerian man would accept that child. Every time you see her you will remember what happened. Tufiakwa!'

'Think about it carefully. When you love someone you can make exceptions. And remember, the idiot who caused it was dead, shot. So, it's not as if he will come back and claim the child.'

'You don't get it Ada. On your wedding day, before you even had a chance. Haba, which Nigerian man would do that? Abeg, no way.'

They parked by the concrete embankment opposite the ageing but still imposing glass-and-steel IMB bank building, and after parting with one thousand each, they went looking for a tent and chairs. The concrete wall had been built to stem the seasonal floods that ravaged Victoria Island. Locals, and those who believed such things, said the flooding was caused by the mermaid who was upset with the bank building. They said the glass panels that covered the walls of the bank caught her reflection when she had her bath and whenever she got angry the beach would overflow and wreak havoc. The stretch of prime real estate from Bar Beach to the television studios right before Silverbird cinema had become a promenade filled with abandoned, rotting houses on account of her rage.

The perennial flooding had also cost Bar Beach dearly; once the weekend destination for families, back when there were no multiplexes, Bar Beach had since lost out to newer, more clement beaches like Elegushi, Lekki, Alfa and Elekan. In the years since the embankment was built however, business had started booming again and the abandoned buildings were being reclaimed.

The beach was also a place of dark history where armed robbers and coup plotters were publicly executed in the seventies. The people of Lagos used to call it 'The Bar Beach Show'. Now, all that was on show were cheap prostitutes hawking diseased triangles, drug dealers peddling Indian hemp, skinny young boys leading skinny horses for hire, white-robed prophets selling prayers, and Olokun worshippers telling auguries while hawkers announced the availability of every item imaginable.

'Tent na five thousand naira,' the skinny young man who led them said.

'Say who die?' Ada asked switching to street-level pidgin. 'We be like oyibo people for your eye? Go bring one big stout, coke and Smirnoff ice jor.'

The young man opened his mouth to speak but Ada's unwavering gaze unnerved him. He laughed nervously. 'Madam na 2K una go pay o.'

They ordered suya, and while they were waiting a young woman came by with a tray laden with stuff: herbs soaked in hot drinks, kolanut, snuff, cigarettes, and things Abel couldn't even identify.

'Oga I get Alamo bitters. If you take am, my sista go happy when you reach house,' she said winking at Abel, who took the small plastic bottle with the green label from her.

'What's Alamo bitters?' he asked Ada, but the young woman piped up.

'It is for waist pain and man power,' she informed him with another wink.

'Oh, an aphrodisiac?' He turned to Ada who had a smile on her face. 'What do I need it for?' Abel asked, reaching out to return the bottle.

'Maybe you will get lucky tonight,' Ada said.

'With who?'

She smiled and opened her palms wide on her lap as if to say, *Search me.*

After the girl left, a tall, thin man in a white soutane approached them, his palms raised in greeting. He had stooped shoulders and a goatee and his huge feet were bare and dusty from pounding the shore.

'Greetings from Jehovah,' he intoned as he came close but Ada waved him away. 'Blessings from Jehovah,' he said, turning away and evincing no iota of disappointment.

He was not gone for two minutes when a dreadlocked Rasta ambled over, a guitar slung across his chest. He was speaking before Abel realised that Ada did not even attempt to shoo him away.

'It is not my express intention to segregate your ambient party but I would like to serenade you both with a song or two in return for some shekels,' he told them, baring nicotine-stained dentition and sounding like a butler from a period movie.

His accent was posh, but he looked like he had just woken up from under some mean bridge in the sadder precincts of Lagos.

'Play me Sting's "Every Step You Take",' Ada said looking over at a perplexed Abel.

The Rasta played the song on cue, the original version, twanging away like he was playing a sold-out stadium, his sweet voice carrying on the cool evening air. When he was done he turned to Abel and said; 'Make a request, dear sir.'

To humour him, Abel said, 'Play me Clarence Carter's "I Got Caught Making Love".'

Abel thought there was no way he would know that song or even sing it but he watched, stupefied, as the guy leaned back, cleared his throat and began to sing, his eyes shut tight. Super impressed, Abel gave him five thousand naira when he was done and the guy bowed and kept bowing until he was gone from sight.

'That was something,' Abel said.

'They call him "Human Jukebox",' Ada explained as their drinks and suya arrived. 'Someone said he used to be big in the US. He came back to Nigeria and opened a club but drink and drugs left him washed up on this beach like so many things and people in Lagos.'

They sat there alone yet surrounded by people, in the waning light of the day, the sound of tyres on tar raging behind them as bankers and sundry corporate types closed for the day and headed out of the island for their homes on the mainland.

It was the daily grind of Lagos. Most people left home as early as 4am from far-flung locales on the mainland in order to beat the morning traffic leading into the island. They would get into the island, then snatch an hour or two of sleep in the car park before work started. At night they would wait till 9pm before they headed home. Lagos was a city of men and women who had forgotten how to sleep and lived out their insomnia in gridlocked traffic.

Abel felt like a decadent impostor as he sat there, drinking his stout, eating suya and enjoying the company of a beautiful woman. Never in his life had he thought this would be his reality. Lagos had been a place in which he never thought he would belong but somehow, on this trip, with its background of pain and anxiety, he'd found a city that welcomed him and made him one of its princes.

His phone rang; it was Calista.

'Are you avoiding me?' she charged, but there was laughter in her voice.

'Absence makes the heart fonder,' he told her and she laughed some more.

'I leave on Monday. We should hang out.' Abel said it was a good idea.

'A friend is taking me out on Friday night. He says we should go club surfing. You want to come?'

'Haven't gone clubbing in ages, but sure. Expect you Mr Dike.'

'You didn't ask me,' Ada said conversationally when his call ended.

Abel turned to her. She was looking at him. Her eyes were hooded so he couldn't see into them and he wasn't sure whether she was upset or not.

'You are …' he began then changed tack. 'I didn't think you would want to.'

'I am what? A married woman? A widow? Which?'

'Ada, don't be like that,' he said, taking her hand. She let him hold her for a while, then pulled away.

'We should be going.' She drained her glass.

He drained his, paid the young man for the tent, the drinks and the suya, then they drove home in silence.

—

Auntie Ekwi arrived before either of them got out of bed the next morning.

'I had a dream,' she began the moment Abel joined her and Ada in the living room upstairs.

'What happened, Auntie?' Abel asked as he sat down.

'I saw Soni. Some men were chasing him. He ran and ran but they finally caught up with him, and then the person in front wasn't even a man. It was a woman, hitting him and screaming, "You lied to me, you lied to me." I woke up and prayed to bind all evil forces. On my way here I dropped by to see the prophet and he said we should come for prayers on Friday night.'

'Friday night,' Abel groaned. 'I can't make it. We have to move it forward to another date.'

'Why? This is urgent,' Auntie Ekwi said, looking from Abel to Ada.

'Abel has to go out of town,' Ada told her. 'We will do the prayer another time.'

'Oh, he is travelling. The journey can't be postponed?'

'No. It has to do with work,' Abel said.

'Work? I thought you are a teacher,' she said as if teaching was not work.

'Yes Auntie, I teach and it can't be postponed,' Abel said pushing the steel into his voice. 'We will do it another time.'

They had breakfast together and before she left with her driver, she took them upstairs and led them in prayer.

As she prayed, Abel remembered her as a young woman who seemed incapable of getting enough sex. She slept with his father's colleagues, their drivers and most of the men in the neighbourhood. His mother suspected for a long time that she was the one who deflowered Soni.

'Once a man says boo, you throw your legs open, eh,' he used to hear their mother berate her. 'Can't you say no?'

It was close to thirty years since the night she left their house, but, he could remember it as clearly as if it had happened yesterday.

At the time they'd lived in a building that comprised two bungalows sitting side by side. The other bungalow was occupied by the bursar. His wife was a vice principal in a girls' college, so didn't live with him. He lived, instead, with his younger brother, who was sleeping with Auntie Ekwi and who they would later catch in his mother's bed. When his mother found out, she forbade Ekwi from ever going into that house. And so she devised other means.

Both houses had pantries at the back. Auntie Ekwi would go into theirs and she and the bursar's brother would make love through the bars on the window. They were at it one evening when Abel's dad discovered them. Auntie Ekwi moved out that same night.

Now she was a prayer warrior with three children and a husband who cruised around Lagos with the car Soni bought her, while she jumped from bus to bus. He was beginning to see a pattern – piety as a means of escape.

Abel didn't go out the next day. After waiting for a while and watching CNN with him, Santos asked whether he could leave. He told him he could.

He swam laps in the pool with Ada and even though she didn't speak much, they were civil, driving out together to go fetch Zeal from school and then to Victoria Island because Zeal kept screaming, 'I want ice cream, I want ice cream!' Ada took them all to an ice cream place off Idowu Taylor.

They watched a movie together when they got back — a biopic of Frida Kahlo, the Mexican artist who lived a tragic, pain-wracked life.

'Wine, anyone?' Ada asked with fanfare as the movie ended. The movie seemed to have cheered her up considerably.

'Sure,' Abel said, bouncing Zeal on his lap — a place that had become his favourite spot.

They sat on the balcony beside the living room upstairs and because it hadn't been used in a while, Philo had to come sweep and dust.

'Go and give Zeal his bath,' Ada said, but the boy refused as he played with Abel's moustache.

'Uncle, bathe me,' he cried over and over again, until Abel had to take him to the bathroom and give him a bath.

When he got back to the balcony Ada had already poured a drink.

'You got a Chianti,' he said, pouring for himself.

'Yes. I sent for it.' She smiled broadly. 'I enjoyed it.'

'Did I tell you how I got to know about it?'

She nodded. 'The movie *The Silence of the Lambs*'.

'Ah,' Abel cried in mock horror. 'One of the signs of old age; you start repeating stories.'

'True. Been meaning to tell you.' When Abel looked up sharply in shock, Ada laughed. 'Just kidding.'

The view from the balcony was lovely. It looked out onto the waters and Abel was sure that with a pair of binoculars he could see all the way to Falomo Bridge.

'I didn't know we had such a view.'

'Soni liked to sit here and read the newspapers while he drank cognac. He used to call himself a grandee and spoke about buying a boat but never got round to it.'

Abel was silent as he took in the information, a shy smile playing around the corners of his mouth.

'Did I say something funny?' Ada asked.

'No. But these days when you talk about Soni, it sounds like you are talking about someone else. The Soni I knew never had time to read the newspapers. Whenever he opened one it was to read a cartoon. When we were much younger, he loved *Garth* in the *Daily Times*, and then *Modesty Blaise* when there was still *New Nigeria*.

'As we got older, Soni's taste evolved to *Mr and Mrs* and then *Kaptain Afrika* in *Vanguard*. Sometimes it was *Obe Ess* in *The Guardian*. He had no time for news.'

'Well, he used to sit out here and read the papers. Maybe age mellowed him,' Ada said.

Abel nodded in agreement. 'I would have loved to see that new man he became.'

They lapsed into silence and Abel watched a gaggle of geese fly by in formation, their wings flapping as if synchronised.

'Soni used to love birds when we were kids. He once owned an eagle called Pokey.'

'Yes, he told me that. I wondered at the name – Pokey of all things.' Ada laughed.

'I guess he already knew he would poke his way through life,' Abel told her, laughing too.

They lapsed into silence again, each lost in what Abel supposed were recollections of what Soni had meant to them as individuals.

'I have been meaning to speak with you regarding some developments on Soni's case,' Abel began. He had been seeking the right moment to bring her up to speed. The Bar Beach had looked like a good place but things had soured towards the end.

'You have updates?' She set her glass down.

'Yes. My friend, Calista, the lady that dropped me off?'

'Yes?'

'She works for the Lagos State Government.'

'Wow, that was Calista Adeyemi?' Ada exclaimed. 'I thought she looked vaguely familiar. She is a Lagos Big Babe,' she said and Abel marvelled all over again how everyone in Lagos just seemed to know who everyone else was. 'I hear she is very close to the governor.' Ada added with wink.

'Oh really? She is very close to me too,' Abel told her and laughed.

'You are a Lagos Big Boy too. So, what did she do?'

'Well, when I bumped into her at Silverbird and she asked me what I was doing in Lagos, I told her about Soni.' Abel related the chat with the CSO and the commissioner, his visit to Panti, the change of officers in charge and the arrests.

'My God Abel, you can kill. You are so secretive. How come you never mentioned all these?' she asked.

'I wanted to have something concrete. I am really sorry about that.' He told her about the man who stole Soni's chequebook and how they were all finally arrested alongside Nicole.

'My God. Dr Nicole? I knew your brother was fucking her but I liked her. She is very elegant and pretty.'

'Well, that's where we are.' He picked up the glass she had just topped up, ignoring the remark about Dr Nicole.

'Wow, we may have to tell your mum.' Ada stared into the distance. 'Dr Nicole is very popular among Lagos Big Girls and Boys. Once the press learns that she is at Panti, Soni's name will be dragged into it. Jesus, I just hope the press don't get involved because then your mother will hear.'

—

Nnamdi had asked that they meet at Bogobiri, on Maitama Sule, off Raymond Njoku in Ikoyi.

'I don't know where that is,' Abel told Calista when they got into his car.

'It's not hard to find. It's a lovely place. Quiet, arty, nice food, cold drinks, lots of white journalists, and music, some days. I had an interview there once with some Kenyan journalist from the *FT*.'

She was right. It was not difficult to find.

Abel drove down Falomo Bridge, descending right as if to Bourdillon, then made a left and took the roundabout into Awolowo Road. Driving past the Church of Assumption on the right, he took the first left at Calista's prompting and then made a right about forty metres in.

Bogobiri was jumping. A band was set up and Nnamdi's massive bulk filled out a semi-circular seat. He was dressed in baggy denim trousers and a big polo top that hid his paunch. He was dining with a petite woman who looked young enough to be his daughter. The girl was pretty and eager in the way Lagos girls are; overdressed and over-made-up, with wandering eyes and legs that parted easily.

Beside Nnamdi and his guest were four white men, an elderly white lady and about four other Africans. The room was thick with cigarette smoke.

'This is Calista Ade—' Abel began but Nnamdi shushed him.

'My God, what is a commissioner doing with a pauper?' He rose and took Calista's outstretched hand.

'Senior special assistant,' Abel corrected him.

'Nonsense, what do you know? SSA is a cabinet position. She is the same rank as a commissioner. Sit, sit my dear and tell me how you met my poor cousin.'

'Poor *older* cousin,' Abel said as he sat down.

'This poor cousin of yours is one of my best friends ever,' Calista told him.

'Wrong choice, wrong choice,' Nnamdi muttered shaking his head. 'That was because you hadn't met me. Now that you have met me that mistake must be amended.'

'Oh, for once I agree with you,' Abel said raising his voice because the band had started up. 'You are a mistake that must be amended.'

The ladies laughed while Abel and Nnamdi slapped palms.

'Would you believe it, we made bets that Abel wouldn't live beyond secondary school and I lost,' Nnamdi said.

'Why did you do that?' Calista asked.

'I was very sickly as a boy,' Abel explained. 'It was a running joke. No one thought I would live past secondary school.'

The waiter arrived to take their orders and Nnamdi remembered to introduce the girl; her name was Mimi, he said.

'Nimi,' the girl corrected and Nnamdi laughed.

'Old age, it happens to all of us. Nimi is with us on industrial attachment. This is part of her induction.' He winked at Abel, who shook his head.

They drank and ate pepper soup. At about eleven, Nnamdi said they should all go in his car.

'My driver will drive. You can leave your car here. We will pick it up on our way out.'

Abel, Calista and Nimi sat at the back while Nnamdi rode in front with his driver. The spacious Lincoln Navigator smelt new and the leather felt almost downy, like you were sinking into cotton wool.

'Take us to Diablo,' he told the driver.

'This car is lovely,' Abel complimented him.

'Na for show, my brother. Don't be deceived,' Nnamdi said and Calista laughed.

'Double N, we know your story,' she told him.

'Which story? Don't tell me you believe all those lies in the press about one billion naira? If I see one billion naira I will faint. In short, I will go into a coma.'

'But you won't die,' Abel jibed. 'Greedy man.'

'Die? How about you who got to heaven's door so many times and refused to go in? Go and sit down my friend.'

Diablo was on Awolowo Road, adjacent to Keffi Street and right beside a Diamond Bank branch. The snout of a danfo bus was sticking out of the wall on the floor above, which housed a boutique.

It was a small, packed space with an odd assortment of patrons; banker types who still looked stiff and formal even though they had taken off their ties and jackets, and a motley crop of young boys with too much money and skinny jeans that sagged. Then there were the girls: young, nubile, scantily clad and shaking things all over the dance floor.

They had wine and liqueur racks on both walls. Music was blasting and people were dancing around tables and in the inner space. A table was quickly arranged for them and when the waiter came by Abel asked for a shot of Hennessy.

'Bottles,' the young lady said.

'I don't need a bottle,' Abel responded, shouting to be heard. 'Just a shot.'

'Get us a bottle of XO,' Nnamdi said tapping Abel on the arm and pulling him close. 'They only sell by the bottle.'

'Really?' Abel asked surprised. Even though he now had access to more money than he could spend, he was often surprised when it came to spending it.

'Yes. You come here when you are really thirsty,' Nnamdi joked. 'Don't worry, I will share the bottle with you.'

They ate asun, peppered and barbecued goat meat that made your tongue sing and your eyes water, and while the ladies drank red wine, Abel and Nnamdi ran through the cognac. Twice, Abel got up to dance to D'banj and Tuface with Calista.

There was an informal air to the place that made Abel feel at home. He didn't know exactly how to describe it, but it looked like a wine shop that had been magically transformed into a nightclub.

A squat, heavily built man wearing dark glasses that looked like a huge eye stood by the door like some modern-day Cerberus, letting people in and occasionally denying some. Abel took it all in as he sipped his cognac, wondering who was who in this wild place and what fantastic backstories they all had.

He was speaking to Calista when Nnamdi jumped to his feet and saluted.

'My general, I remain loyal.'

'Double N! So somebody can see you like this without visa?' A tall, dark-skinned man had walked in on the arms of two scantily clad girls. He hugged Nnamdi.

They shook hands all around, Nnamdi's introductions lost as the music came on again.

As they sorted out their seating Nnamdi motioned to the girl who had served their drinks.

'Put two bottles of Moët Rosé on his table and add it to my bill.' He leaned in between Abel and Calista. 'He is ex-militant. He got a huge contract last month to guard vessels and base stations. Huge contract.'

'But not as huge as one billion naira?' Calista asked with a teasing laugh.

'Madam Commissioner, don't believe rumour-mongers, I beg you,' Nnamdi said, wagging a finger at her.

'Double N, may your billions never finish,' the general called as the waitress set down two ice buckets with bottles of champagne in them.

'Billions, where did you guys see this billion, eh?' Nnamdi asked, and they all laughed.

Two of the general's men had now joined him at the table, and the waitress was setting down flutes when a young man with sagging pants bumped into her as he staggered past and upset the whole arrangement. The flutes and the two bottles hit the tiled floor and a pool of pink fluid massed.

Nnamdi was on his feet just as one of the men reached for the boy who had caused the accident and began to throttle him. 'No problem, no problem, get two new bottles,' he said, freeing the boy from the grip of the ex-militant.

'Money man!' the general hailed Nnamdi as they shook hands again. 'It is a good thing to have billions.

When Nnamdi headed to the gents, Nimi leaned over to Abel and Calista and said, 'Four bottles of rozay – that's one hundred and seventy-four thousand naira in less than five minutes. People have money in this country o.'

Nnamdi and Calista exchanged glances but said nothing.

From Diablo, Nnamdi asked his driver to head to La Casa, which squatted by the water next to the Civic Centre, just across the street from 1004 where Calista lived. And it was on the drive there from Diablo, with Nnamdi snoring softly, that Calista told Abel the story of Nnamdi's one-billion-naira contract.

A fluke, everyone said, but Nnamdi had managed to propose some innovative deal to the top four GSM companies all at once on behalf of some Chinese company. The deal had sailed through and people said he got a cool 10 per cent from the ten-billion-naira deal.

'He really made one billion naira?' Abel asked a bit too loudly.

Nnamdi woke up. 'Don't mind them Chiedu; it's all rumours. If I had one billion naira wouldn't I be the one sitting at the back with the pretty ladies?'

Everyone laughed and then lapsed into silence as the beast of a car purred up Falomo Bridge.

There was a police checkpoint where Nnamdi's driver called out 'Yellow' as if that was the code word for the night.

Atop the bridge, with the water stretching out on both sides and the lights shimmering on its undulating surface, it struck Abel, forcefully, that Lagos was a lovely city if only it could be quiet and clean and calm for a moment. But then he shook his head and laughed softly to himself. Make the city quiet and clean and calm and it would no longer be Lagos.

Lagos, named by the Portuguese after the lagoon that girded its waist, was like a river swollen with flood and every time it threw up there was chaos. That was what made it Lagos; the wild garden where men and women came to harvest dreams, some lean and some bounteous.

THE LIGHTHOUSE

Abel spent all of Saturday with Calista. They had been too tired for anything more than a kiss when Nnamdi dropped them off at about 3am after a wild time at La Casa and another bottle of cognac.

'Your car will be here before you wake up,' Nnamdi told them.

'Ask for Williams at the gate. Give him the car keys,' Calista told the driver. 'Tell him it's for me.'

She was up by the time he roused, pottering around in a G-string and nothing else.

'Good morning,' he said as he walked naked into the bathroom, preceded by an early morning erection.

'There's a spare toothbrush,' she called out to him.

He could smell frying eggs by the time he had brushed and showered.

'Eat, you need your strength,' Calista teased as Abel came and kissed her from behind, his hands cupping her breasts.

'This food will go cold, but you know this one is always warm, so eat.'

Abel had a huge appetite. It was always that way. Most times he didn't realise how hungry he was until he took the first bite.

He helped her clear the dishes and even though he had already had his bath, he joined her in the shower, lathering her body all over. They both fell, wet and naked, into her bed.

'I wish I didn't have to go, but his Excellency would be mad.'

'His Excellency?' Abel asked.

'Yes, the governor. The state is subsidising my fees at Harvard. I have a scholarship but it doesn't cover everything,' she told him as she played with the hair on his chest.

'And I hear you guys are an item,' Abel said casually, looking up to catch her reaction.

'An item? Me and the governor?' She sat up.

'Yes. I hear you guys are really close.'

'I have heard that myself. You know, once you are a woman doing well, you have to be sleeping with the boss. The governor is my cousin and I am sure you remember him; he used to send me money when we were in school. I sent you to his chambers once and he gave you these crisp naira notes that you stole half of. You remember?'

Abel remembered. 'I didn't steal half. I exchanged half.'

'You stole,' she teased, hitting him with a pillow.

'Really, that's the governor? ' Abel said pinning her down. 'I never made the connection.

'It's OK. I have heard a lot myself,' she said and took his left nipple between her teeth.

Abel jerked at the sudden nibble. 'That was painfully sweet,' he said, pulling her down on him. He loved to run his fingers down the length of her body. If he had any talent for drawing, he was sure he could draw her from memory.

There wasn't an ounce of fat on her body back in school or even now. Calista was one of those women who could eat anything and not pile on the pounds.

'Maybe pregnancy will change all that,' she'd told him the last time he brought it up.

'You are a beautiful woman.' He stopped his trip around her body to nuzzle her neck.

'And you are my fine bobo,' she said, straddling him. 'How is Mr Man doing; is he asleep?' Abel eased up to give her access. 'Good boy.' She inhaled deeply as she took him all in.

She had mentioned The Lighthouse a few times and that afternoon she insisted they visit before she left Nigeria. So, after lunch and another shower, they drove out of 1004 in their separate cars, Calista in front and Abel behind, down to the Ajose Adeogun roundabout and onto the street everyone now called Zenith Bank Street because of the number of Zenith Bank branches on it.

Calista made a right after the imposing glass–and–metal Zenith Bank head office building and Abel followed. They drove past the Halliburton office and made a left into Sinari Daranijo, a somnolent street.

'That's the club that used to be run by the lady who was murdered in 1004,' she told Abel, pointing as they made to cross the road. 'It used to be called Club Q.'

The Lighthouse seemed like someone's residence. There was a long white building to the right and another at the end but in the space in between and to the left were long benches and tables set as if in a private garden. There was also a well-kept lawn.

A gaggle of men and ladies were seated around the tables and on couches made out of cane and raffia. There were also high stools on which were perched patrons smoking long cigars and drinking wine or cocktails. The whole scene reminded Abel of something out of a movie or a novel.

'Isn't this someone's house?' Abel asked as a well-endowed young lady dressed in flowing boubou came up to welcome Calista.

'We haven't seen you in a while,' she said after they hugged.

'Work, travel, work,' Calista sing-songed, and the lady laughed, her face glowing.

'Hello, my name is Uzoma,' she said to Abel, extending well-manicured fingers. 'Welcome to The Lighthouse.'

'Abel.' He shook her hand. 'Thank you.'

They sat on a comfortable couch. 'You like palm wine?' Calista asked. 'Haven't had it in years, even though I live in the bush,' Abel answered. 'Let's have it.'

While they waited for their order, a slim, bushy haired man dressed Fela Kuti style in tight-fitting clothes wheeled out a loudspeaker. He set an iPod on top of it and, a moment later, Fela's deep voice took over the space.

'That's her husband, Tayo,' Calista told Abel and waved.

Tayo strolled over. 'Where you dey since?' he asked in pidgin as he and Calista hugged.

'Busy, work.' She pointed to Abel. 'My good friend Abel. I brought him here to experience The Lighthouse.'

'Tayo,' he said with a wink at Calista as he took Abel's hand. 'Thanks for coming.'

'My pleasure,' Abel said.

His grip was firm and he looked very fit.

'Tayo does yoga. I come for sessions here sometimes. You should try one. It helps you relax.'

They drank their palm wine and Abel watched the place fill up. Smart young men and women walked in and ordered the most incredible things: garri and groundnut, zobo and asun, roasted banana and groundnut, palm wine and barbecued fish.

'I need to buy something to travel with. Uzoma makes these beautiful designs,' Calista said, taking him by the hand and leading him into the white building.

Inside, Abel was awed. He picked up a few of the flyers arranged on a table by the door. On one, Tayo was bent double, face buried in his knees in a yoga pose. Abel knew it was him from his hair. There were announcements for a reggae jam session the following night and something about a reading by award-winning author Sele Bature. Abel remembered reading reviews of her novel *Sandflies*, and making a mental note to order it so he could teach it. That thought seemed like it had occurred to him a lifetime ago.

Inside and to the left was a boutique selling everything from wristwatches to bags and clothes Calista said were from Uzoma's labels, Cheetah and Skanking. There were flowing jersey gowns in bright colours for women, tie-dyed embroidered tops for men, as well as T-shirts and old-school skirts and tops made from lace.

Something about the place made Abel want to spend the whole night there, especially when he went to use the restroom and found a stack of books sitting on a side stool by the door.

'Are these for sale?' he asked the cashier at the counter.

'No. You can sit and read while you do your business.'

Calista bought two tops and a heavily embroidered top for Abel.

They kissed for a long time at his car and he promised to take her to the airport on Monday evening.

'First I will fly to London to spend a few days with my mom,' she said as she got into her car.

'Monday evening then,' Abel said and waved.

—

He spent the next day with Zeal. They played and watched cartoons together until the boy fell asleep on his chest his drool leaving a wet patch on his T-shirt.

'You are good with children,' Ada told him as Philo scooped up the sleeping Zeal and took him upstairs. She was dressed in her favourite denim cut-offs and a colourful Ghanaian danshiki top. She had no bra on and Abel glimpsed the side of her breast when she moved her arm.

'Yes, I like kids,' he said.

'Yet you haven't made any, or are you hiding a brood in Asaba?' She prodded him playfully with her foot.

'Haven't been that lucky, my sister. Blame it on condoms.'

Two of her friends had visited while Abel had been playing with Zeal and left just as Zeal was falling asleep. 'My friend likes you,' she told Abel.

'Which one?'

'Helen. The dark, tall one.'

'She looks like a man.'

Ada laughed so hard she fell off her seat. 'Na wa for you. You are scared; not man enough?' She wiped away the tears, showing skin.

'No, but I like my women feminine, petite. Not with more muscles than me.'

'She has got a lovely body. You should see her naked.'

'You really are serious?'

'Yes. She is a widow with a son and she has a good business. Loves to read and watch movies too. You guys would be good together – now that Calista is leaving town.'

'And you think she likes me like that?'

'I don't think. She told me.'

'Really? You guys talk about such things.'

'Really. Of course we talk about such things, silly.'

Abel was quiet for a while. What was Ada playing at? Why did she think she needed to hook him up? Had her friend really expressed interest in him?

'Next time, she comes, introduce us,' Abel said, looking up at Ada. 'Maybe we could hang out. But first, I need to take you someplace this evening.'

'Where? Not another restaurant. You will make me fat and Soni will kill you when he gets back,' she said, then the realisation dawned and she sat back on the couch and bit down on her palm.

'Let's keep hope alive.' He touched her lightly on her knee.

She didn't say anything in response so he rose to go upstairs. '6pm, ok?'

She nodded and said nothing, tears falling down her cheeks.

—

The Lighthouse was packed when they walked in. A band had been set up on the concrete slab beside the lawn. Tayo was singing a Bob Marley tune and the patrons were catcalling and clapping as they walked in.

'Ada, been a while,' Uzoma said, hugging her.

'Hello,' Uzoma said to Abel, clearly trying to recall his name.

'Abel,' he said and she nodded with a smile.

'Calista just left,' she whispered and sashayed off.

'You cheat,' Abel said punching Ada lightly on the back. 'Why did you act like you didn't know this place?' Abel asked as they found seats.

'I didn't want to spoil your surprise.'

It was a beautiful night. The band would play a tune and then someone from the audience would take the mike and sing. Some would stop halfway, the words lost in the labyrinthine whorls of time, and the audience would join in, everyone laughing and having a good time.

A lady went up and sang a Steel Pulse song with Tayo backing her. Then, to Abel's amazement, Ada jumped onstage and sang Bob Marley's *Redemption Song* in a beautiful voice that had everyone clapping and the band giving her a rousing drum roll.

'We are full of surprises tonight,' Abel told her as she returned to her perch.

'We try to please,' she said with a girlish laugh.

YAWA DON GAS

Lagos was in a foul mood that Monday morning. The sky was overcast and had the look of a bitter woman with a grudge. A brewing storm threatened rain.

'I think Zeal should stay home,' Ada said to Philo as she led a fully dressed Zeal downstairs.

'I want to go!' the boy cried.

'It's going to rain,' Abel told him. He was watching CNN while sipping coffee.

'I like rain,' Zeal squealed and made a dash for the door. Philo grabbed him and dragged him, squealing and laughing, back to his uncle.

'Let's watch Teletubbies,' Abel said, tickling him.

'School!' Zeal cried, giggling and struggling to wriggle free.

That was where they were when Santos burst in, wet from the rain. He had eight soft-sell magazines with him.

'Bros, yawa don gas. Sabato gist is all over the papers.'

Ada cried out and dashed into the living room. Santos spread out the papers on the floor. The stories were all the same, with slight variations.

Top female banker arrested over missing businessman
Lagos Big Boy missing, top female banker nabbed
Top female banker arrested in connection with missing businessman
Sabato Rabato missing; Top female banker detained
Lagos Big Girl, Dr Nicole, in police net for fraud
Where is Lagos Big Boy, Sabato Rabato? Police seek clues
Is Sabato Rabato dead? Fear grips Lagos socialites
Sabato Rabato feared dead. Associates nabbed

'We must contact Mama,' Ada said. 'Before someone tells her.'
Abel smiled his thanks. Ada always thought fast. He had been paralysed by all the stories.

'Yes, I will call my sister right away.'

Abel called Oby and briefed her. 'Go to Uncle Mezie. Tell him what has happened and let him go with you when you tell her. When you get to mummy, call so we can also speak to her.'

When Abel dropped the call, he replied to a text sent by Auntie Ekwi. She had a Bible passage for him as usual: *God is our refuge, an ever-present help in trouble. He is our strength we shall not be moved. It is well and I will send a text to the Prophet to pray for us.*

After sending his reply, Abel considered all the papers spread out in front of them on the floor. The story was all out: Dr Nicole's arrest, the forged cheque and Soni, who some reports said had been missing for months and hadn't been seen at any recent social events. The kicker was the one that read, *Sabato Rabato's pretty wife has been seen around town with a handsome young man and tongues are wagging.*

'"Handsome young man and tongues are wagging?"' Abel exclaimed.

'You are handsome and you are young, aren't you?' Ada said and told him to calm down. 'Soft-sell stories are all about innuendo and speculation. At least we know who the handsome young man is. Let the tongues wag.'

Abel scanned the papers again and exhaled loudly. 'How did they even find out in the first place?' he asked no one in particular.

'Soni's girlfriend, Dr Nicole,' Ada said as she paced. 'If he had kept his dick in one place most of this wouldn't have happened. Nine inches my arse!'

Abel looked up at her, considered saying something, then thought better of it. He could tell she was hurting and that was her own way of letting off steam.

'And bros, more papers will come out tomorrow,' Santos said. 'Soft-sell papers come out on Mondays and Tuesdays.'

Abel growled as if in pain and placed both hands on his head. This was becoming a circus he hadn't planned for. 'What do we do now? Send a rejoinder, call a press conference?'

'Press what?' Ada stopped in front of Abel. 'You don't even respond. Give it one week and they move on. Someone one else will disappear. Some rich man will sleep with his daughter or a huge scandal will break out in Abuja and they will forget all about Sabato Rabato.'

'But we won't forget,' Abel said, marvelling at how analytical and in control Ada appeared, as if this was something she had anticipated.

'We will never forget,' she said and continued pacing.

Abel's phone rang. 'Oby.' he said, expecting to hear his sister's voice, but a man answered.

'Is this Mr Abel Dike?'

'Who is this?' He paused to look at the caller ID. He did not recognise it.

'My name is Uzor Arinze. I am a reporter with *Oui International*. I am calling about your missing brother. Is it true that his account officer has been detained with regard to his disappearance? Were they lovers?'

'Who gave you my number?' Abel barked. 'Do not call me again. Ever!' He cut the call.

They were relentless. When he wouldn't pick up, they called Ada. When neither responded, the text messages came flying in like a swarm of locusts.

About two hours later, the doorbell rang. Philo answered; a short lady with red lips and kinky dreadlocks was standing at the door.

'My name is Monica Dimka. I write for—'

'Shut the door, shut the door!' Abel screamed at Philo.

He was losing it, his hands shaking badly. How had the dwarf made it past the gateman?

His phone rang just then and he was reaching out to put it off when he saw Oby's name on the screen.

When he answered, his mum was crying and screaming: 'I told him to stop o, I told Sunderland to stop. Chukwu nna, what am I going to do?'

The voice faded; Oby must have moved some distance away from the tumult.

'I am with Mummy,' she said. 'She has been rolling on the floor since.'

'What did you expect? Is Uncle Mezie there?'

'Yes.' Abel asked her to put him on.

Uncle Mezie was their mother's brother, a no-nonsense retired teacher.

'Chiedu, what is this that I am hearing?' he asked in Igbo.

'Uncle that's what we met in Lagos,' Abel replied in the same tongue.

'When did this one happen?' Abel explained quickly. 'You people can kill o. Something like this happened and you kept it under your fingernails for over two months. Chiedu, my son, is this a good thing?'

'Uncle, do not be offended,' Abel placated him. 'We did not want anyone to worry. We thought this would be sorted out quietly.'

'You do not want us to worry, eh? What is a father's job if not to worry? Chiedu, this is not good.'

Abel apologised again, and charged him to take care of his mother, who was bawling uncontrollably in the background.

There were more calls and text messages but Abel and Ada ignored them all. The next call he took was from DSP Umannah.

'I have been trying to reach you all day,' he said as soon as Abel answered.

'It's been crazy down here,' Abel told him.

'I know. I saw the papers. Welcome to Lagos my brother,' Umannah laughed.

'It would be funny if it wasn't so terrible. That banker got us into this, I tell you.'

'Yes, yes. She moves in the top social circles – the so called Lagos Big Girls.' Umannah hissed. 'But don't worry. It's a circus and it will soon move on. Lagos is like that. I will keep in touch.'

Abel finally went up to shower before going down for lunch. Then he sat downstairs and read all the papers from beginning to end, astonished at the details in some and amazed at the complete falsehoods in most.

Some of them read like fiction. Some reports said Soni's car had been found in a ditch on Victoria Island. Others said Lekki. Most of them got the make of the car wrong and many of the papers spelt his name as Sabato Roberto. Many got Ada's name wrong while others said he had two wives, Dr Nicole and Ada.

By evening, Abel's anxiety was easing and he was beginning to find the stories hilarious. There was something about them that seemed calculated to make you laugh, as if they were writing for the shock value.

He was drinking cognac by the pool when a text message came in.

I hv news abt ur broda's whereabts. Reply if u want 2 c him alive.

Who is this? Abel replied, stopping himself from calling the number only by sheer willpower he didn't even realise he possessed.

Mayowa Akindele, came the reply.

And who are you?

I am d publisher of Excel Celebrity magazine. Print and online

And how come you know his whereabouts?

i hv my sources

And who are these sources?

As a professional journalist of over 15 yrs standing, I cannot divulge d id of my sources. I am running out of credit so let me know weda u will come around.

Where?

The address was in a street in Ikeja off the notorious Ipodo, between Olowu and Ikeja bus stops.

Meet me tomoro by noon. Come alone. If u come wit smbody, I will not show. I will take u 2 meet someone.

Abel dug into the pile of papers and found *Excel*. Someone by the same name of Mayowa Akindele was indeed the editor and publisher, but the paper was a trashy little piece of junk. It was filled with typos, from the captions to the stories. It seemed as if the guy wrote the way he typed his text messages, without bothering about spelling or grammar.

'Oga, one man say e want to see you,' the gateman announced. Abel had given him a stern warning after his Monica Dimka slip.

'Who is it?'

'He say his name is Nnamdi.'

Abel asked him to let his car in.

Nnamdi was all smiles as he came out of the Prado.

'Knowing that you are a poor man, I came with my own drink,' he said waving a bottle of Courvoisier XO.

'You are a true son of your father,' Abel said as they shook hands.

'I saw the papers. I knew it would be madness so I said let me come down and wipe your tears.'

'God bless you.' They settled at the pool and Abel passed a clean glass to Nnamdi.

'I didn't realise there had been some arrests,' Nnamdi said as he sipped his drink.

'Yes – that banker lady and some lowlifes. I went to Panti. It wasn't them. They were greedy idiots but they had nothing to do with Soni going missing,' Abel explained.

'And the lady?'

'The greediest of the lot. You know her right?'

'Like Abraham knew Sarah.'

'Looks like I am the only one who never got there. You remember the day we met at the bank?' Nnamdi nodded. 'I had been to see her.'

'I was on my way to see her. She must love guys from our place.'

'I suppose so. Anyway, we had finished talking when she just hit me with, "I know your brother is missing, but he promised me a new car for my birthday and it's not as if he is broke." I was completely shocked.'

'Why were you shocked? In Lagos the hustle never sleeps. To her, Sabato is missing and so what? She also told me about her birthday when I went up. It's a hustle my brother.'

Abel digested the information slowly. It made sense, even if in an amoral kind of way. Everyone knew how Soni had made his money and he was sure everyone felt they had a right to some, if only they could find a way to get their hands on it.

Had he got in on the hustle too? Was that what he was doing by entrenching himself in Lagos and digging deep into Soni's wealth and home? There he was, lying in a lounge chair by the pool, sipping fine cognac. Was he not feeding off Soni's hustle by sleeping in his bed, driving his cars, wearing his clothes, enjoying the company of his wife? What made him different from Dr Nicole? Soni was missing, yes, but the party was still in full swing.

'Sorry, what did you say?' Abel asked. Lost in his thoughts, he had missed the question Nnamdi asked.

'I said, have you guys told your mum? She will hear now that it is all over the papers. Your mother and father loved to read papers. I remember, whenever I came to your house, your father would ask me to sit and read the newspapers while someone went to fetch you. I hated those moments, especially when you didn't come out immediately.'

Abel said his mother had been informed and that Oby was keeping an eye on her.

Ada came out then to greet Nnamdi.

'Our fine wife, how are you?'

'Fine bros.' She curtsied. 'You abandoned us.'

'How can I? How is the boy? I haven't been here since his naming ceremony. Lagos swallows you.'

'Is it Lagos? Or have you been busy counting your money?' Ada teased. 'We heard stories o.'

'Rumours. All rumours.'

Ada asked after his wife and kids then told them to have fun.

'How are your parents?' Abel asked him. 'Your mum was a very pretty woman but she was wicked, o. Her flogging was something else.' He recalled Nnamdi's mother, who had taught them geography and wielded a mean cane.

'She is fine. She and my dad are in India. She was having issues with her waist so they went for surgery. My sister Nkechi is with them too.'

'Money is good.'

Nnamdi sat up with a smile. 'You know, I still remember the slap my father gave me when I came home with my first car, a Peugeot 505. "No son of mine will be a 419 criminal," he spat and threw me out. Remember, it was in your house I spent that Christmas. I went legit because 419 almost destroyed our generation. I got into telecoms the moment I saw the opportunity. Soni couldn't drag himself away.' There was something that sounded like regret in his voice. 'We always envied you, you know. How you stayed away and didn't even come to Lagos. Did I tell you what happened when I got to Lagos? I wrote to Eva. You remember short Eva with the big head?'

'Yes, I remember Eva. Where is he now?'

'Dead. He was beheaded in Saudi Arabia. When things went bad here and money ran low, he got into the drug trade.' Nnamdi refilled his glass. 'Anyway, I sent word to him that I was coming to Lagos and could I stay with him? You know Eva couldn't say no to anybody. He said sure, so I came. Big mistake. There were five other boys from our set staying with him. It was a tight space. At night we would talk and argue and some people would quote Karl Marx and Adam Smith, Frantz Fanon, Steve

Biko, Albert Camus, Jean-Paul Sartre. Imagine us all: white-collar criminals spouting revolutionary rhetoric. It was funny. But Eva always had the last word. After we had all poured out our frustrations with revolutionary quotes as footnotes, he would unroll his thin mattress, and as he stretched out for the night he would say, "I will make it in this Lagos like Malcolm X said, 'by any means necessary.'" And every time he said that, someone, I think Ralph, would say, "You know, it was actually Jean-Paul Sartre who coined that phrase," and then everyone would shout him down with, "Shut up, you told us before."

'Those were crazy nights. If anyone had made some money during the day, he would buy drinks. The preferred drink was Squadron because it was cheap and gave a quick buzz. You remember Squadron, abi? Many nights, the landlord, tired of our arguments would bang on the door and tell us to shut up. "Una dey crase! Omo ibo buruku. People want to sleep o." That was where it all started. Then we branched out and things changed and, you know, but my parents never accepted me. I would send money and they would send it back. Intact. You teachers, eh? Anyway, my mother took ill. I went to see her and, would you believe, my father wouldn't let me into the house. My mother wouldn't see me either. They wouldn't accept my money. I came back to Lagos and cut off all ties with my 419 cronies. Telecoms had just started and I invested all my money. Many 419 boys invested in politics and telecoms and many lost out big time. But I was lucky and God started blessing my hustle and from there things changed. I wish Soni had done the same, you know, made a clean break, but then I suppose he had got in too deep. Your brother made serious money. He was a wealthy man and now it's all coming to you; you who never got your hands dirty. Life is funny, my brother.'

They sat there by the pool drinking and reminiscing until late. They recalled the old days when their parents all lived in the same compound. How Abel and Nnamdi's fathers would play tennis together on Wednesday evenings and Saturday mornings.

'I wanted to be them, in their white shorts and tops with your father's red headband.'

'But you were too skinny,' Abel teased, and Nnamdi laughed.

'And you were always at death's door.'

'But my father still took me. I played tennis.'

'I played football and I also played with the girls. You, we thought you would die a virgin.' Nnamdi poked him playfully in the ribs.

It wasn't until 11pm when Nnamdi was leaving and asked after Calista that Abel remembered.

'Damn, she leaves tonight. I was supposed to take her to the airport. God. Drive safe, Nnamdi. I need to call her.'

Her flight was for 10.45pm. There was no way he could meet her.

'I was too upset to call. I didn't think you would forget,' she told Abel when she finally picked up after the sixth call, and only after he had sent a text explaining what happened.

'I am really sorry but it's been a crazy day.'

'You could have called, sent a text. I would have understood.'

'I am really sorry.'

'It's OK. I have to board now. Our flight was delayed. Your mum knows now, right?' Abel said she had been informed. 'Good, she doesn't have to hear it from the press. And someone is taking care of her?'

'Yes, my sister. Oby, you remember her. She came to visit once when we were in school.'

'I remember. She had lovely long hair and she caught us in bed, once. We had a good laugh afterwards. She was born-again, right, and she didn't find it funny.'

'No, she didn't. She told me you were a Jezebel and you would lead me to hell. They caught Soni with girls all the time and said nothing, but it was *me* who would go to hell.'

'Jezebel indeed,' Calista said with a laugh. 'See, I have to board now. Take care of yourself and when this is all sorted out you should come visit me. You can afford it.'

Abel said goodbye and went upstairs. He showered, brushed his teeth and got into bed, but sleep was a distant country. He lay in bed, trying to make sense of what he was becoming. Or had become. The things Nnamdi and Calista said had unsettled him. Were they seeing things he had refused to acknowledge, the fact that he had assumed what was not really his?

'You should come visit. You can afford it,' Calista had told him. Nnamdi had said, 'He was a wealthy man and now, it's all coming to you; you who never got your hands dirty. Life is funny, my brother.'

It was true; he hadn't engineered Soni's disappearance but he hadn't wasted any time taking over all that Soni left behind. There was always money in his pocket now. He had spent more money in the past two months than he had ever seen or had access to in his entire life.

As he lay there in the dark listening to the music filtering out of Ada's room, his thoughts running in different directions, a passage from Achebe's *Things Fall Apart* came to mind. He didn't remember the lines verbatim but it had something to do with an Igbo saying about the relationship between the hero and the coward.

Soni's life was epic and heroic; a full book brimming with grand tales and multilayered chapters. His own, by comparison, was a mere paragraph, the words scrambling around like excited ants, trying to find their niches. His life had become, as Achebe wrote, the coward's house from where people stood and pointed to the crumbling ruin of the dead hero's abode as they said to their children: that was the house of a great warrior who is no more. Soni was the hero, and Abel was under no illusions who the coward was.

EVERYTHING IS ~~not~~ ABOUT MONEY

He woke up the next morning with a blinding headache. He hadn't slept much and he needed painkillers. He rummaged through the dresser and cupboard. There was nothing, so he sent Ada a text. She knocked about ten minutes later and walked in with a pack of analgesics.

'Good morning, my husband,' she said as she handed him the plastic pack.

'Someone is in a good mood today,' Abel said as she fetched a bottle of water from the fridge, poured and passed it to him.

'What happened? You had a fight in your sleep?' She settled into the couch.

'No. I didn't sleep well, at all. My mind was wandering.'

'I hope it didn't wander into my room. I was stark naked.' She laughed.

'Don't worry. It didn't.' He flicked the remaining drops of water in the cup at her.

They were quiet for a while and then she spoke.

'See I have been meaning to ask you something,' she began, leaning towards him, so close he could see the top of her breasts. She must have felt his eyes on her because she leaned back again.

'Yes?'

'Well, it's over three months now since Soni disappeared and I pray every morning for him to come back and be father to his son and a husband to me. But with every passing day I realise that we may never see him again. I know so many people who have been swallowed whole by this city.' She got to her feet and began to pace. Abel had noticed that Ada liked to pace whenever she had something she felt needed to be said.

'I am talking of young girls, mothers, fathers on their way to or from work and school. Abel, these were ordinary men, good people. With Soni, it's a lot different. We know what he did, we know he had enemies and if they have kept him for this long without asking for money they will never let him go. So, I need to ask you; if Soni doesn't come back, what happens to us? Are you going to stay on with us? Will you go back to Asaba? He has legit businesses and you can help run them. You are a smart and intelligent man. But I need to know. My family has asked me the same question and now I am asking it of myself; if my husband never comes back, what happens?'

She had stopped mid-stride, one foot in front, the other behind, as if poised for lift-off. Her face was partly in the light and partly in shadow, framed, as it were, in a penumbra of anxiety, and it gave her a surreal aspect. She was bouncing on the toes of her right foot and breathing fast from her mouth as if the effort at speech had sapped her.

'Ada, I don't know,' Abel began tentatively. 'I like to make plans, but this time I have no idea what to do. I agonised over how to tell my mother but somehow, circumstances sorted it out.

As to what you ask; let's wait and see what happens, especially with the story now in the papers. But just know that whatever happens I will be here for you and Zeal.'

Ada did not speak; she just stood, her bosom heaving as she bounced on her feet. There was a knock and Abel asked the person to come in.

'Good morning bros. Iyawo good morning,' Santos greeted as he stepped into the room. He had more magazines and newspapers. 'It's now in the serious papers,' he said handing them over to Abel. 'And it is all over the internet.'

That was when Abel remembered his appointment with the journalist, the mysterious publisher who had called from *Excel* magazine to say he knew where Soni's whereabouts.

He showered, had breakfast, listened to CNN for a while, then texted the journalist at about 10.45am.

Just leaving Lekki now. Are we still good for noon?

There was no reply and when it was almost 11am Abel got into the car and asked Santos to head to Ikeja. He was close to the gate when a message came in.

Pls call me. It was the journalist.

He told Santos to park while he made the call.

'Sorry, I couldn't call. No credit,' he said breathlessly as if he had been running.

'No problems. So, what's up?'

'We can't do noon. I have a meeting with a client for noon. It wasn't planned but I have been chasing this deal for a while. Let's do 4pm.'

'Same place?'

'No. A different place. I will text you and remember come—'
Abel cut him off before he finished.

They drove back home and he watched a movie, *Happy Feet*,
with Zeal who was home because Ada wanted to avoid what
she said would be a circus at his school.

'I don't want people looking at me. You know they all read
soft-sell papers and then pretend they don't.'

'Hypocrisy of the rich and famous,' Abel said.

'Well, you are one of us, now,' she told him, and Abel felt
something give way in the pit of his stomach.

His reverie was broken by the buzz of a text from Calista.

*Arrived safely and been gisting with my mum since I got home.
I sent you a gift, something to upgrade you into the 21st century.
An aide will drop it off. Can you imagine; one day gone and I am
in tatters. Miss you, Mr Dike.*

Abel read the text a few times, then sent a reply.

*The past few weeks have been heavenly because of you. Miss you
more, Miss Adeyemi.*

A while later, he called Santos and asked him to get the car
ready for his Ikeja appointment. They left the house at 2pm.
It was a bright, sunny day and Abel knew that without traffic
they would be in Ikeja in an hour.

As they turned on to the Third Mainland Bridge from Osborne,
Santos cursed and swerved to the right, but it was obviously too
late. Abel felt the impact and then they were skidding. Santos
fought to keep the BMW X5 straight. He won, bringing the
car to a rest by the edge of the kerb, just.

They got out of the car to inspect the damage. A danfo bus had hit them from behind, shattering one of the tail lights. The bus was now sitting in the middle of the road, its passengers disembarking in a hurry from fear of being run into by an oncoming vehicle.

As Abel and Santos approached the bus, the passengers all pointed in the distance. Abel followed their lead and he could just make out two men, one in shorts and the other in buba and sokoto, running as if the devil was chasing them. It was the driver and his conductor.

'They said you will arrest them,' one of the boys who had just got off the bus said and Abel burst into laughter, the tears coursing down his face as they inspected the damage before continuing with their journey.

He knew why they were running. Where or how in God's name would they find money to fix a BMW? Fear had given wings to their feet.

———

When they got to Ikeja, they parked at Mama Cass on Allen, and while Santos waited, Abel took an okada, the ubiquitous motorcycle taxis with demoniac riders who, because they got into nasty accidents on such a regular basis, had been designated a special ward at the orthopaedic hospital. The riders were usually young boys, always high on something, or old men with poor eyesight who drove bikes as a side gig. They weren't the most adept or careful riders.

'Abeg, don't drive too fast,' Abel said as he perched behind the driver. He had already given him the address for his rendezvous and negotiated the fare.

The driver mumbled something as he handed Abel a dirty helmet, which passengers were required to wear by law.

The location was an open-air beer parlour. Plastic chairs were arranged four to a table; all of it branded by one lager or the other. A big-screen TV hung precariously from the wall and as Abel sat down and ordered a beer, he began counting mentally to see how long it would stay up before it came crashing down.

He had counted to 560 when someone settled into the seat beside him.

'Mr Dike? Don't look at me, please, just pick up your glass if it's you,' the voice said and Abel reached for his glass.

'You are Mayowa, right? And you said you know something about my brother?' Abel asked, speaking with his lips hovering over his glass.

'Yes.'

'OK, what do you know and what do you want?'

'I don't want anything. I just want to help a young man like myself,' he said. 'I think I know the people who took your brother. I met someone who can help you find them.'

'Why doesn't he go to the police?'

'Police? Why? I thought you wanted to find your brother?' Anger and impatience crept into his voice.

'Yes, I want to find my brother.'

'Then why are you talking about police? I am only trying to help. I heard something that will benefit my fellow man and I decided to help.'

'How much do you want?' Abel asked, turning ninety degrees to look at the guy. If he was paying, he needed to see who he was paying.

He was surprised: Mayowa didn't look like much. He was a thin man with beady eyes. His face would have been handsome but for the ravages of time and circumstance. He looked to be in his late thirties, about Abel's age.

'Everything is not about money,' he said. 'Can I order for a beer?'

'You can order for ten,' Abel blurted before he could stop himself. He waved the waiter over.

The guy gave Abel a look that conveyed both irritation and resignation as he asked for Gulder. He was either shameless or really in need of a drink.

'Bros, everything is not about money,' he repeated, his tone softening, all talk about Abel not looking at him gone. He poured his drink, took a large swig that emptied half of the glass and then smacked his lips and rubbed his palms together. He was thirsty.

As Abel looked at him, he could see his life story written all over him. This was a blind mouse, like millions of others nosing their way through the underbelly of Lagos, hoping for the lucky day when they would score some cheese. Most of them came to Lagos with a vow, like Eva, to make it or die trying. Most of them died, trying.

He could see the grime around the collar of the long-sleeved shirt he had folded to the elbow, revealing gaunt arms that ended in bony fingers with dirt underneath the nails. His shoes were tucked under the table, out of sight, but Abel could guess that they were dusty from tramping through the streets, looking for the 'hammer that would bring the Hummer'.

'See, let's stop beating about the bush; what do you know and what do you want for it?' Abel asked, laying his cards on the table.

'I met someone who knows something and he is the one who wants something too. Me, I have human sympathy. Today it is you; tomorrow it can be me. No need chopping from somebody's bad luck.'

Abel ignored the platitude. 'Is the person here?'

'Yes. He is watching to make sure you came alone.'

'So, are we going to meet him?'

'Yes, but we have to agree first. Then I will send him a text and he will reply.'

'So, how much?'

'He said one million naira.'.

Abel did not betray any emotion as he turned to him and asked: 'Have you ever seen one million naira before in your life?'

Mayowa swallowed hard, his Adam's apple bobbing. It was almost hard to believe that he was just drinking beer. He seemed to be choking on something solid.

'Bros, it is help, I came here to help,' he said, looking Abel in the eyes.

'And what will he give us?'

'He said he knows who took your brother and he knows where to find them.'

'So, how do we do this then? Even if we could pay, I don't have a million naira with me here.'

'How much do you have?' Mayowa's eyes glinted.

'About ten thousand naira.'

'Hmm, I am not sure that will work o. This kind of transaction is cash and carry. The man is scared and he wants to use the money to travel.'

'Where?'

'Abroad. He is taking a big risk in talking to you, you know.'

Abel told him he would pay 500,000. Mayowa asked for 800,000. They haggled and though Abel waited for him to send a text message, Mayowa did not. They finally settled for 600,000.

That was the first inkling Abel had that something was not right, but his brother was missing and how could one ever be sure what was real and what was not? It was all shadows. He would rather he did something than give in to his doubts.

'You will drop advance payment,' Mayowa said.

'Advance?'

'Yes. The man has to know that you are serious.'

'But you said I should come alone and I did. Why does he want advance payment?'

'The man has to know that you are serious,' Mayowa repeated as if he was talking to an idiot who wasn't paying attention and had difficulty understanding simple things.

'I told you; I have only ten thousand naira here and we haven't paid for our drinks.'

'There are ATM machines; you are a Big Boy. You must have an ATM card.'

Abel paid for their drinks, then walked with Mayowa to a bank on Toyin Street. He withdrew one hundred thousand naira, which was his limit and gave it to him.

'The man would have preferred two hundred thousand naira,' Mayowa said as he pocketed the money. Then, looking up with a smile and rubbing his palms together he asked, 'Nothing for the boys?'

'What?'

'I am just a messenger. Won't you find me something for transport?'

'Excuse me?'

'Bros, this money is not for me. It is for the contact. I am not charging you but I spent my money to get here just to help a fellow man.'

Abel gave him five thousand naira out of what was left in his pocket.

'I will text you at night to give you directions as to where we will meet again. God bless you.'

Abel watched him walk away, his dusty, worn shoes clinking against the macadam as he crossed the street. Then Abel flagged down an okada that took him back to Santos at Mama Cass.

When he got home, there was a package waiting from Calista. Inside was a Blackberry and an embroidered tie-dye top from The Lighthouse. There was also a card that had 'To my Main Man' on its cover. Inside, Calista had written, 'A Blackberry for you, caveman. Lose that old phone.' Abel smiled as he pulled the phone from the pack.

'You are the only thirty-seven-year old I know who doesn't have a smartphone or a Facebook account,' Calista had teased him that night as they left La Casa. Abel had been asking how she coped with her Blackberry beeping all the time.

He inserted the battery into the phone and plugged it in to charge. Santos would help him sort it out the next morning. For now he waited, jumping every time his old phone beeped, but he did not receive a text message from Mayowa. When he got tired of waiting and called, Mayowa did not pick up. The next time he tried, an automatic message told him the phone was switched off.

'Maybe he has drunk himself into a stupor,' Abel consoled himself.

He didn't have dinner. He ate some biscuits and drank a beer. He was lying in bed and reading when Ada knocked and entered.

'Do I put on the light?' He said yes. 'You didn't eat dinner?'

'No. I usually don't eat dinner, actually. You are going to make me fat.'

'Well no one would say I was not a good wife,' she said, settling into the couch.

'No one would say that,' Abel agreed.

Ada noticed the Blackberry pack and reached for it.

'So, we have a Blackberry now? I always wondered when you would ditch that phone.'

'Calista sent it to me, but I will miss my old reliable.' He kissed his old handset.

'You should take it to Onikan.'

'Why? What's happening in Onikan?'

'The museum. It's an antique.'

Abel sat up. 'Is everything OK?' There was something about her that didn't seem right, despite her jokes.

'No. I've been having these nightmares. I thought I could sleep here tonight.'

'Sure. I will take the couch,' he said, getting off the bed.

'I don't stink, Abel.' She rose and crossed the room to his bed.

'Is this a good idea?' he asked, feeling himself react. He just couldn't help the effect she had on him.

'Just create some space for me,' she said as she got in. 'It's a large bed.'

Abel switched off the room light but left his reading light on. He had his book open but he couldn't concentrate. Ada was lying beside him and he could hear her inhale and exhale. He had moved close to the edge of the bed to create some space between them but there was no denying the electric charge on that bed. Tired of trying to concentrate on the novel, he put off the lamp and crept under their duvet. Their feet touched and he pulled away.

Ada was asleep, her breathing even. Abel listened to her breathe, watching the rise and fall of her bosom from the light that came in from the bathroom. He was a man impaled on the flagpole of desire.

She stirred and reached out for him. 'Don't leave me, please,' she whispered, and pulled him close. Abel was not sure whether she was speaking to him or lost in some dream.

—

It was already bright when she awoke in a panic. The clock said it was 6.45am.

'Oh my God, Philo. I don't want her to know I slept here,' she cried as she jumped out of the bed.

'You can take the connecting door,' Abel told her.

'Oh my, I hope I didn't lock it from behind.' She turned the key in the lock. The door yielded. She pulled it open and there on her bed, were Philo and Zeal. Abel turned around and bit into his pillow.

Ada avoided him the rest of the morning and when Philo served him his breakfast, he could have sworn she had a knowing smile playing around her lips. Or maybe he imagined it, his guilt making him paranoid. Still, he didn't like the fact that Philo had seen Ada leave his room clad in her nightgown. Nothing had happened, he knew, but who would believe it? Even he had a hard time believing it.

Santos helped him transfer his contacts from the old phone to the new one, then helped him set up his email accounts, Blackberry Messenger, Facebook and Twitter.

'Bros, you are now connected.' Santos handed him the phone.

Abel thanked him and sent a text to Calista.

What's your BB pin, darling?

Wow, someone has been upgraded, Calista replied.

Santos was out to buy fuel when Ada came downstairs to sit beside him.

'Zeal is driving me crazy. He wants to know why he is not going to school.'

'He can go back tomorrow.'

'I wanted him to sit out the whole week. But yes, I will take him,' she agreed. 'You sorted out your Blackberry?'

Abel nodded. 'Santos helped out.'

'And where is he?'

'I asked him to fill the tank and buy me some stuff from Shoprite.'

'OK. You need to change all your passwords, you know. I don't trust Santos. Let me show you how.'

She helped him change them and left to make lunch.

Abel dialled Mayowa's number for the sixth time that morning but he didn't pick up. He sent a text: *Mayowa, waiting to hear from you. What's the next move?*

He didn't get any reply, so later that evening he sent an angry message: *Mayowa, what's going on? Suddenly, you can't take my call because you have money in your pocket.*

That elicited a response. *Pls don't insult me, Mista man. I told u I am only trying 2 help. d man said d money you dropd is 2 small and how doz he know u will pay d rest. He said I shd send u dis acct no.*

Abel looked at the account number and felt like strangling someone. 'Bastard!' he screamed.

Ada came out asking what the problem was and as he told her the story she started laughing.

'Abel, he has "jobbed" you,' she said, wiping her tears on her sleeve.

'Jobbed me how?'

'The money is gone. He screwed you. That's what 419 guys call local. You are his mugu.'

'It can't be. I will get him.' Abel reached for his phone sent him a text.

I don't want to pay any money into the bank. Let's meet somewhere and I will hand over another 200,000 naira. Then when we are done, I will give him the rest.

The reply was instant. *I will call u 2moro 2 let u know. Let me spk 2 d man 1st.*

He didn't call back or text that day nor the next. Seething, Abel told Santos.

'Bros, the man has jobbed you,' Santos told him 'You don fall mugu.'

'It's not possible,' Abel insisted. 'He is the publisher of a magazine.'

'Publisher?' Santos burst into laughter. 'Bros, that money is gone. E don go. The man don do you local,' he said in pidgin.

Abel could not, did not, would not accept that he had fallen prey to a conman. This was a story he had read about for years; how conmen would promise a million things and deliver nothing. He never thought it could happen to him.

'Santos, see his office address is here in the magazine. We will go and see him tomorrow.'

'OK. You want to go with police?' Santos asked in Igbo.

'Yes. I will call Umannah and tell him to send us one of his men,' Abel said, suddenly feeling in control.

'OK, and how much did you give him?'

'One hundred thousand naira.'

'And where is the receipt?'

'Well, he didn't … Erm, I didn't ask for a receipt.'

'Oh, so you will tell police that you gave him one hundred thousand naira just like that and you didn't ask for a receipt. Who was your witness?'

'It was just two of us at the ATM on Toyin Street. A Skye Bank ATM. I remember.'

'Clap for yourself, bros. See, if you involve the police, they will just chop from two of you. That guy won't even sleep in the cell for one night. That's what police will call; your word against his. You will say you gave him one hundred thousand naira and he will say you are lying. Police will ask you for your witness, you will say it was just two of you. Police will say the onus of proof rests on you. Have you heard police quote the law before? Don't let police quote law for you, bros. You won't like it.'

The more he thought about it the more he began to realise that Santos was right: he had been had by the dirty, stinking conman posing as a journalist. He thought he had read him well that day as a man on a hustle but his concern over his brother had switched off his alarm system.

'Two things you must know is this,' Santos said, switching to English like he always did when he wanted to sound intelligent, then messing up his grammar in the process. 'Two things can make it easy to job somebody. The first one is greediness. If a man is greedy, you can job him just like this.' He snapped his fingers.

'The second thing is desperation. If a person is desperate for something, just like you who wants to find his brother. You can do anything and guy man can job you just like that. It's like a woman that is desperate for a child; any fake prophet can fuck her.'

Abel glanced at Santos for a moment, amazed at how his mind functioned and wondering why, if he was such a fount of wisdom, he was still working for Soni and earning eighty thousand naira monthly.

'OK, so what do we do? Just let him go with the money, just like that?'

'Ehen, bros. Now you are talking. We will go and see him and if we catch him, I swear, he will vomit that money.'

When Ada brought him dinner, she set the food down and said, 'Food is served, Uncle Mugu.'

'Very funny.'

'But how could you have been so gullible?'

'I was desperate. I thought he was telling me the truth. I didn't realise he was leading me on.'

'Beer or wine?' She opened the fridge.

'Just water, my sister. I am tired of everything. Everybody in Lagos is out to get you. And you know, after I gave him the money, he turned to me and said "God bless you."'

Ada sat down and regarded Abel like a mother addressing a dim child. 'So, what next?'

'Santos says we should go and see him. Make him "vomit" the money.'

'Tough guys. You should take it easy o.'

Abel ate with appetite. When he was done, he went upstairs, showered and got into bed with a novel. His phone buzzed with a message from Calista.

♡✴╾°╌╼♡✴ Calista €♡✴╾°╌╼♡╍: *whassup, mister dike?*

ABEL: *I am ok. How are you?*

♡✴╾°╌╼♡✴ Calista €♡✴╾°╌╼♡╍: *luvly. What's good?*

ABEL: *nothing much. Just got conned out of 100k.*

♡✴╾°╌╼♡✴ Calista €♡✴╾°╌╼♡╍': *wow, welcome 2 las gidi. how did that hap'n?*

ABEL: *some journalist guy called to say he had a source who had information about Soni and that i should pay 600k. I paid a 100k advance and i think it's gone.*

♡✴╾°╌╼♡✴ Calista €♡✴╾°╌╼♡╍': *he got u gud.*

ABEL: *yes, he did. So, how is your mum?*

♡✴╾°╌╼♡✴ Calista €♡✴╾°╌╼♡╍': *Mum is gud. Chillin. Took her shopping 2day. All she bought was a pair of slippers. Funny woman. What r u up2?*

ABEL: *in bed.*

♡✴╾°╌╼♡✴ Calista €♡✴╾°╌╼♡╍': *with ur sister-in-law?*

ABEL: *very funny.*

♡✴╾°╌╼♡✴ Calista €♡✴╾°╌╼♡╍': *just checking. out of sight, could be out of mind, honey. I've seen it b4.*

ABEL: *you didn't see it here.*

♡✴╾°╌╼♡✴ Calista €♡✴╾°╌╼♡╍': *true dat. Need some excitement?*

ABEL: *Where? How? It's late and I told you I am in bed.*

♡✴╾°╌╼♡✴ Calista €♡✴╾°╌╼♡╍': *wait a second. Sending you sth. Just accept, ok?*

ABEL: *ok.*

Abel waited a while and then a file came through. He accepted and opened it. Calista was topless with just her hand shielding her breasts.

Her next message flashed on his screen.

♡☀︎⌣⋯☞♡☀︎ Calista €♡☀︎⌣⋯☞♡⌣: *u likey likey?*

ABEL: *you are crazy*

♡☀︎⌣⋯☞♡☀︎ Calista €♡☀︎⌣⋯☞♡⌣: *crazy 4 u. So u like?*

ABEL: *nice'*

♡☀︎⌣⋯☞♡☀︎ Calista €♡☀︎⌣⋯☞♡⌣: *just 9ce?*

ABEL: *Very nice.*

♡☀︎⌣⋯☞♡☀︎ Calista €♡☀︎⌣⋯☞♡⌣: *cool. If u r a gud boy, i will send u anoda tmao. Cool?*

ABEL: *cool.*

♡☀︎⌣⋯☞♡☀︎ Calista €♡☀︎⌣⋯☞♡⌣ : *Sleep tight, boo and here is one more 4 d road.*

About two minutes later, his phone buzzed, and when he picked it up, there was a picture of Calista topless, her breasts hanging low, like ripe fruit, but her face wasn't showing.

'Bad girl,' Abel muttered, as he enlarged the picture.

———

The office was off Olowu street in a big two-storey building that was a riotous warren of offices and residences. There seemed to be a million burglar-proofed doors festooned with stickers from the religious to the political and the unapologetically commercial.

Jesus is the answer

Where will you spend eternity?
Vote PDP
Eko oni baje
APC is the party
Fashola is working, Lagos is working
Alamo Bitters na the baba

Apart from the rash of stickers, Abel noticed many drooping wires hanging from doors, eaves and roofs like tired, emaciated snakes.

It was the sort of building that made Lagos what it was: a city bursting at the seams with people. Mayowa's office was hard to find and they had spent close to ten minutes walking up and down before they finally found a door with an *Excel Magazine* sticker.

'It must be here. Now the dog will vomit that money,' Santos said as he turned the handle and pushed at the door. It didn't open.

'Knock. Say you want to place an advert,' Abel told him, while he stepped out of sight, down the stairs.

Santos knocked but no one answered. 'Bros, nobody is here.' Abel was walking up the stairs when Santos motioned at him to wait.

'Who are you looking for?' a voice asked. Mayowa; he would know that voice anywhere.

'Is this *Excel Magazine*?' Santos asked. Mayowa replied that it was.

'I want to place an advert.' Abel knew that if Mayowa didn't bite Santos was likely to say something that would give them away.

'Is it product or public announcement?' Mayowa rattled the chain to get the door open.

'Em, na advert for house.' The door creaked open. 'Na you be the publisher editor?'

Mayowa answered, then uttered a sharp cry as Santos struck him. Abel bounded up the steps, slammed the door shut behind him and latched it using the chain and padlock that was still dangling. Blood streamed from Mayowa's nose.

'Santos stop. How many people are here?' he asked Mayowa as he pulled him up from the dusty rug and propped him against the wall.

'Only me.'

'Where is your artist? We want to place an advert,' Abel mocked. He asked Santos to look around the office.

'Nobody is here,' Santos confirmed when he returned to the room.

It was a small place with just two rooms; Mayowa's office and an outer one that served as reception area.

Abel studied him. His shirt was already stained with blood but it was clearly new. He had on a brand new pair of shoes and there was a gold chain on his wrist.

'Where is my money?' Abel punched him in the face.

'I don't ha—'

Santos kicked him hard in the stomach. Mayowa gagged and sank to the floor.

'Where is the money?' Santos asked again.

'I spent it,' Mayowa said, curling into a ball. Santos directed a well-aimed kick to his head.

'So, you think you can job my bros?' Santos asked, kicking him with every word.

'Sorry, sorry, sorry,' Mayowa was crying, the pain making him slur.

Santos stripped Mayowa of his wristwatch, phone, bracelet, shoes and necklace. He placed the shoes on the table and stuffed the rest in his pocket.

'I thought you are a publisher; why did you do this?' Abel asked, stooping to hear him.

'Bros we are all hustlers. Who doesn't want to hammer like your brother?'

Abel regarded him for a while, then straightened. Mayowa looked like he had been run over by a car. His left eye was already swollen and he was bleeding from his nose and mouth. His new shirt was dusty and bloodstained. He didn't look good.

'Santos, let's go.'

Santos shook his head. 'If he starts screaming thief, we are dead. Let's tie him up and cover his mouth.'

They gagged Mayowa and tied him to one leg of his table with his belt. As they made to go, Santos said, 'Bros, give him one for the road.'

Abel looked from Santos to Mayowa. There was fear in the publisher's eyes and a silent plea too, but Abel remembered how he had strung him along; how he told him about the mysterious stranger who knew Soni's whereabouts; how he had taken the one hundred thousand naira and then asked for something for the boys; and how he said 'God bless, you' and crossed the road, probably whispering to himself and smiling at how easy and gullible Abel had been.

Anger bubbled to the fore. He lashed out and kicked Mayowa in the gut. Mayowa screamed as bloody snort bubbled out of his nose, tears clouding his eyes.

'That's my bros,' Santos said as they headed out. 'Leave the door open, so someone will see him.'

Abel was tingling all over and his heart was pounding. He felt alive. He hadn't been in a fight in years. Not that what had happened back there could be termed a fight, but it had been good to give as good as he got. He had lost one hundred thousand naira but that wasn't what it was about. It was the insult of being had by a man purporting to help. He felt good that he had stepped up to the plate and said, *you don't mess with me*.

'Bros, I didn't think you could do it.' Santos said as they made a right at the roundabout that led to Allen and Opebi. There was respect and admiration in his voice.

'Why?' A sharp thrill coursed through him; he had acquitted himself well in the eyes of his younger cousin.

'Bros, you na gentleman. Na we be street boys.'

Abel smiled to himself as they waited at the traffic light, pleased to have done something tangible. True, he was a gentleman, and all his life he hadn't been in more than three fights because there was something about hitting and hurting another human being that made him recoil.

But that afternoon Abel had been ready to kill. Something had snapped in him and all the impotence he felt since arriving in Lagos and not being able to do anything to find his brother had bubbled over into rage in Mayowa's office.

'Where's that Fela CD?' he asked, rummaging in the glove compartment.

'It's here.' Santos fished it out of the side pocket of the door.

Abel slotted it in and selected track six, 'Palaver'.

———

He showered when he got home and was surprised to find his hands shaking. His knuckles were bruised. Now in Lekki, with the adrenaline rush gone, he was suddenly back to his old self – the analytical, rational man.

He wondered how Mayowa was and whether someone had found him and freed him. It wouldn't be nice to leave him tied up for long in that state. He and Santos had done some damage. Abel was suddenly overwhelmed by fear; what if he didn't make it? What if they had done much more damage than they had planned to? He thought about that last kick and rolled out of bed.

He pulled open the cabinet and poured himself a Scotch. He downed it in one gulp and stood up, remembering that Mayowa's phone and things were still in the car. The phone could be traced to Lekki if someone called and it rang. He went downstairs, dismantled the handset and took the SIM card to the kitchen, where a bemused Philo watched as he fried it to a cinder over the flame from the gas cooker. He went back upstairs and dropped the empty hand set in the drawer of his dresser.

Abel sat down on the couch. Where had all that rage come from? He knew now, with the excitement gone, that he had lied to himself in the car. It wasn't about the money and it wasn't even about the insult of having been conned. Something was changing inside him. Living in Lagos, he was beginning to act in ways that were completely alien to his personality.

He drank some more Scotch, then switched off the light. Sleep didn't come, so he put on some music and lay there in the dark, praying that Mayowa would not die.

Morning brought no respite. He had a hangover from drinking too much, too fast the night before. The box of painkillers was still on the dresser, so he popped two caplets in his mouth and tried to sleep again, but it was no use.

He showered, hoping that cold water would help ease the hangover and clear his head. He had breakfast with Ada, who was full of questions about their visit to Mayowa, but Abel only let on that they had given him a few slaps and warned him off.

'Wow, I hope he won't come after you guys,' she said.

Abel looked up from his plate. He hadn't even considered that. He had been so sure that Mayowa would be so scared he would never make contact again.

'I don't think so,' he said, affecting bravado he didn't feel. 'We made it known that we weren't people he could mess with.'

'Good. I didn't think you had that in you, Mister Lecturer.'

Abel could feel the respect in her eyes and at that moment he realised what his brother had seen in her. Beyond her obvious beauty, Ada was a woman who could be counted on when things got hairy. Abel had seen her take charge, her analytical mind working. She knew what kind of businessman Soni was. She had always known that the situation in which they now found themselves was a possibility and she had been prepared for it, although she hadn't figured that Soni would have his brother as next of kin. Without him in the picture, Abel was convinced that Ada would have taken charge completely. He understood, also, that when she asked questions about what to do, she was not really asking questions but directing him in ways she thought they ought to go.

'Well, I guess a man has to do what a man has to do,' he said, flushed with pride despite his misgivings.

'That's the kind of man I like,' she said and rose as Philo came to clear the dishes.

—

Things returned to normal.

Zeal went back to school. Abel and Ada went swimming at the club and watched movies at the cinema. In the evenings they sat on the balcony and drank wine. Santos handled the clearing and sale of the goods with the buyers paying into a new account Ada had advised they open so they could have access to cash unencumbered by legalese. And though he waited for Mayowa to call threatening fire and brimstone or worse, nothing happened.

With school reopening in two weeks, Abel wrote a letter to his head of department explaining his situation and asking for some time off. He despatched it by DHL.

Ada had been right: the news cycle was done in one week, but they bought the papers anyway just to be sure. Abel was surprised at the way the magazines had moved on as if the previous week hadn't happened. He had expected a follow-up, but there was nothing.

Santos told him *Excel Magazine* wasn't on the stands and for a moment, Abel regretted having taken Mayowa's phone. He could have called the bastard, even if to issue a threat. But it was probably all for the good, he reasoned; a clean cut.

To ease the tedium of his days, Abel finally agreed to a date with Ada's friend Helen. They had dinner at a Korean restaurant in Victoria Island. She talked about her late husband and her son, who was some kind of child prodigy. At nine, he spoke four languages, could play the violin and piano and was already taking guitar classes.

'He will take care of me when I am old,' she said, maternal pride lighting up her face.

Ada was right; Helen read widely and loved movies. She was big on Toni Morrison and Salman Rushdie, and liked movies by Pedro Almodóvar, of whom Abel had only heard.

'We should go see a movie, sometime,' she told him as he walked her to her car.

'Yes, we should,' he agreed as he gave her a peck.

He called her up two days later, more out of courtesy and because Ada made him. They went to see *This is War*, an action-comedy that left them laughing hard with tears in their eyes. They had a drink afterwards and when he walked her to the car she surprised him with a kiss.

He liked her and enjoyed talking to her, he told Ada, but she didn't do it for him.

'I thought it was women who talked and thought like that?' Ada told him, surprised. 'I thought men just stuck it wherever they found a hole.'

'Well it has to be hard enough to stick someplace.'

'Sad. She really likes you.'

Abel's head of department called the next day to say he could take one month off without pay. Abel thanked him and later shared a celebratory drink with Ada.

Things continued in that quotidian manner until Tuesday morning, when Santos sauntered into the dining room during breakfast.

'Philo, get another plate for Santos,' Ada called out, but he hadn't come to eat.

'Abel, we need to talk.'

They both looked up in surprise. Santos never called him Abel, always 'bros'.

'What's wrong with you?' Ada asked.

Santos was whistling and picking his teeth. 'Ada, excuse us.'

Her jaw dropped.

He placed a soft-sell magazine on the table. The screaming headline and rider made Abel die a million times as he read it.

WHO KILLED MAYOWA? Excel Magazine *publisher found beaten to death in his office!*

Ada snatched the magazine from the table and read the caption. 'Is this why you have lost your manners?' she said to Santos in Igbo as she turned the pages. She read the story out loud and each word was like a stab in Abel's gut.

> Mayowa Akindele, the amiable publisher and editor-in-chief of *Excel Magazine,* was discovered dead in his office three

days ago. Initial police reports indicate
that he was beaten, tied up and left for
dead. His body was already decomposing
when it was discovered by neighbours,
who alerted the police. The police are
asking for members of the public with
information to contact their hotline.
Mayowa is survived by a wife and son.
He cut his journalistic teeth at the
defunct *FAME* magazine and launched *Excel*
two years ago, after a stint with a
public relations firm. Reactions have
been pouring in from colleagues who are
shocked at his brutal killing.

Abel was breathing hard by the time Ada was done. He thought
he would throw up.

'So, what do you want now?' Ada asked turning to Santos.

'Fifty million naira and the X5,' Santos said without missing a beat.

'After all these years.'

Santos nodded. 'Yes, after all these years.'

'We can't get fifty million naira from the bank,' Abel finally
managed to say. He was a mess. His hands were shaking again
and he didn't trust himself to get up.

'Yes, you can. We have over seventy-three million in the
new account we opened. Just make the transfer to this account.'

Abel picked up the piece of paper with Santos' account number, his eyes burning with tears. He and Ada would have to sign the cheque.

Ada looked from one man to the other. She rose and told Santos to get out of the house and go to the police. Santos staggered to his feet, his face a mixture of rage and confusion. This was not in the script.

'What will you tell them, eh? Let me hear it,' she asked advancing upon him.

'I will tell them everything!'

'Then why are you still here? Go on and don't come back. You no longer work here. Go to the police but remember we have the money and we have the lawyers and we can fuck you up.'

She flung a teacup at him, raving mad now, with eyes blazing and hair in disarray. She looked to Abel like a deranged Medusa with a full head of hissing snakes.

Santos ducked again as another teacup flew at him, and ran to the door. 'You don't know me, Ada. You don't know me. You are playing with fire,' he said from a safe distance.

'But at least you know me and you know what I can do,' Ada screamed and threw another teacup. It shattered against the door.

'Witch! Wicked woman!' He ran out as she advanced.

'Open that gate and let him out,' she yelled at the gateman. 'If I see him in this house again, you are dead. You hear me?'

Abel was standing by the dining table and watching Philo clean up the debris when Ada strode in and walked straight upstairs.

The blinds were drawn and the room was shrouded in darkness when he stepped into her room. He switched on the light. She was slumped on her pink couch, her head in her palms, crying softly. Her whole body trembled from rage as he settled beside her and pulled her to himself.

'What are we going to do, Abel?' she wailed. 'What kind of wahala is this?' He held her close as sobs wracked her slim frame.

Abel realised at that very moment that he had rounded a bend and there was no going back. So many things had changed and he had to change along with them. A man was dead and he was culpable. He had to fix that and fix the Santos problem too. He knew who to call.

'Everything will be alright,' he said, and he had never meant anything like he did those words.

DUSTBIN ESTATE

Abel finally came to a quiet realisation about Lagos; a disturbing truth that had been niggling at the edge of his mind. It revealed itself to him as a city of dissemblers, and he had joined them in that dance of dissemblance. Everyone was hiding some deception that would, like a pebble flung against a mirror, shatter the image of their fake lives.

For two days after the Santos debacle, Abel and Ada stayed indoors. They spent most of the time upstairs. They had left firm instructions with the guard not to let anyone in. The house help was also barred from leaving the premises under any guise.

They seemed to be waiting for something to break and it got to a point for Abel, where anything would have sufficed: the police, Santos, Soni walking in with two heads. He would have been glad for anything to break the tedium of the slow hours.

But nothing happened. Santos didn't call and neither did the police. Even though it made Abel happy and relieved, there was still some residue of fear, as if the calm was no more than the compressed moment between the flash of lightning and the thunder.

He read books, watched movies, played with Zeal and chatted with Calista. She had arrived in Boston and was busy trying to settle in at Harvard, although she still found time to send him pictures from the shower.

Abel hadn't told her about Mayowa. For once, Ada was his only confidante and he knew the secret would probably die with him, her and Santos. How did one send a lover a text to say *I killed a man last week; beat and kicked him to death with my bare hands and feet*? It wasn't going to happen.

Helen called a few times asking him out to the movies or a reading but Abel always found an excuse at the last minute.

Then Auntie Ekwi called on Thursday night to say she would be coming the next day. She breezed in early that Friday morning in her Ankara gown and head tie of the same material, all of which smelled faintly, as always, of camphor.

'This night vigil is still pending, you know. Our brother is still missing and as the Bible says, we ought to pray and not faint. Are we ready for tonight?'

Every time she walked in that early in the morning, Abel would remember her mother, his grandmother, who used to sell snuff, tobacco, smokers' pipes and gin. He remembered accompanying her early in the mornings to the houses of those who owed her money. They would arrive at 6am, sometimes a little before. His grandmother would rap on the door with her walking stick and rouse the inhabitants from sleep. They were always upset, but somehow that early morning call and, Abel guessed, the dread of having an old woman wake up the neighbourhood with cries of how she was being driven to poverty by a heartless man or woman, always made them pay up. It must have been from her that Auntie Ekwi learnt how to drop in on people before daylight.

'Auntie Ekwi, we are ready,' he said as he settled opposite her. Ada was already with her.

'Good, good. I shall send the prophet a text. How is Zeal? Any news from the police? We all saw the stories in the paper, but like I told you in my text, Daddy has been unwell. I would have been here since.'

Abel told her it was OK. She had sent texts a few times. Daddy was what she called her husband. He was down with typhoid fever, she said, and she had been playing nurse.

'Our wife, could you please get me some water? Thank you.' The moment Ada was out of earshot, Auntie Ekwi leaned close to Abel and spoke in Igbo.

'Chiedu, what is this talk about her having a boyfriend? It was all over the papers how she has been carrying on with some handsome young man. You live in this house, you are the man of the house; how can you let that happen? The people at home will not be happy.'

Something about her tone, her conspiratorial manner just cracked Abel up and he was still laughing when Ada came back bearing a glass and bottle of water on a tray.

'What's so funny?' she asked as she set the tray down. She poured water into a glass and handed it to Auntie Ekwi who took one sip and spat it out.

'It is cold, chukwu nna. Our wife, please get me warm water, room temperature. My cough has not fully gone.'

'Yes, Auntie.' There were questions in her eyes as she looked at Abel, who just smiled at her as she left with the tray.

'Oh, I have now become Ali Baba, eh?' Auntie Ekwi said to Abel in English.

'Auntie sorry. I am really sorry. That handsome young man is me. These people just write what they like.'

'But that's what you should have said instead of turning into a laughing jackass.'

Ada returned with the tray, poured water into the glass and passed it to Auntie Ekwi.

'Should I go and come back later?' she asked in Igbo, looking from aunt to nephew. She was smiling but, having lived with her for almost three months, Abel knew there was no mirth in it.

'Our wife, please sit down and tell me about Zealinjo. How is he doing at school? I hope he is as intelligent as his father.'

Ada sat down, crossed her legs and ignored the question, a fixed smile on her face.

Breakfast was an awkward affair. Then, when they were done and Abel called on Ada's driver to take Auntie Ekwi home, Ada objected, saying she needed the driver because she would be going out in a hurry. Abel took Auntie Ekwi to the gate where he found and paid for a cab.

Ada was lying on the couch in the living room when he came back in.

'I thought you were going out?'

'I changed my mind.'

'Really?'

'Really.'

He glared down at her, trying to control his rage. 'Ada this is childish,' he told her, and stomped off to his room.

He was taking off his shoes when his door was pushed open.

'And talking behind my back is not childish?' she asked, framed in the doorway, her uncombed hair cascading over her forehead and shoulders.

'Is that what this is about?' He switched on the light.

'Yes. She sends me on the same errand. Twice. So you guys can talk about me.'

'What did you hear?'

'Does it matter?'

'See … You were rude to my auntie and I think you should apologise,' he said as he stood and took her hand. 'Come.' He shut the door and led her to the couch. 'She asked how I could let you have a lover while I was living here.

'A lover!' Ada exclaimed, sitting up.

'Yes, the handsome young man you have been seen around town with, remember?' She grinned. 'Now you see why I was laughing. You shouldn't have treated her that way. Auntie Ekwi can be talkative and troublesome, but she has a good heart.'

'I know, but all this stress is getting to me. I will call her and apologise. We are seeing her tonight too. Don't be angry, handsome young man.'

'It's alright.' He took her hand in his. 'She told me on our way out that Santos called her.'

'What did he say?'

'That you and I fired him for no just cause. How that would never have happened if Soni was here.'

'Did she ask him what he did? Did he say?'

'Of course not. He said something or the other about taking money from Dr Nicole and not washing the car. Something silly.'

'Good. We have to talk now. We need to fix the Santos problem. What do you think we should do?'

'Let's give him what he asked for and let him get lost.'

'No, if you give him money he will blow it and come back for more. We will have to keep looking over our shoulders for the rest of our lives.'

'So, what do we do?'

'I don't know, but we have to find a more permanent solution.'

She left him to his thoughts and long after she was gone, he sat wondering what she meant by 'permanent solution', hoping it wasn't what he felt she meant.

—

On the morning when they were getting ready to leave for the next night vigil, Auntie Ekwi came to them and said the Prophet had been given a word. 'He wants to see you two,' she said.

The Prophet was seated behind the tiniest table Abel had ever seen, in a claustrophobic office that seemed to have been carved out as an afterthought. A noisy fan rotated overhead, ineffectual against the heat.

'You will do saara,' he told them. 'Find at least twenty-one homeless children and feed them for three days. There must not be less than twenty-one. Three days. Then we will return here next Friday for prayers. I see dark clouds and we must dispel them with kindness and giving.'

'How does one find twenty-one homeless children to feed?' Abel asked as they walked outside into the brightening day.

'There is always a way,' Auntie Ekwi said.

'Please help us ask around,' Abel told her as they got to her car. Her husband was still recuperating, so she had driven. 'I have no idea what to do or how to find twenty-one homeless children.'

'I will ask questions,' Auntie Ekwi said as she opened her door. Ada was beside her in two strides and on her knees in a heartbeat, surprising Abel.

'Auntie Ekwi, please do not be offended,' she said in Igbo. 'This whole wahala is beginning to affect me. Forgive me please.'

'It is OK, please get up, get up,' Auntie Ekwi said glancing from right to left in embarrassment. They hugged, and Abel and Ada walked to their own vehicle.

'That was something. I didn't expect you to do that in public.'

'Why not?'

'I don't know. Apologising on the phone, in the house, yes. But in public? I was impressed.'

'I may have my crazy moments but I love your brother and I will do anything to make him happy and keep the peace.'

She pulled out and hit the road with a squeal of tyres.

———

Abel's mobile woke him. He had drawn the curtains the moment they got home, turned the AC as high as it would go, and crawled under the duvet.

It was Umannah. 'We haven't heard from you in a while. Is everything OK?'

'Yes,' Abel answered. 'I just haven't been feeling well. The stress of it all is beginning to wear me out.'

'That happens. I thought we should meet so I can bring you up to speed with what we are doing.'

'Sure. Why don't I buy you lunch today, at 2pm. I will text the address. Is that OK?'

'That will be fine. I will expect the address.'

A message came in from Calista as he sent Umannah the address of a restaurant. It was a short message with a picture of her naked in bed.

Do u miss me d way i miss u? she asked.

Yes, much more than you miss me, Abel replied. *Have been sleeping. Just woke up. How is Boston?* He hit the send button and set the phone down on the rug.

There was a commotion at the door and Abel could hear Philo's voice: 'Come back, here. Uncle is sleeping.'

Zeal. Abel got off the bed, opened the door and asked Philo to let him in.

'Uncle Abel, let's watch *Happy Feet*.'

'Sure.' Abel took the DVD case from him and lopped Zeal on his bed. He put the movie on and went into the bathroom to shower.

He ate a light breakfast in the room, feeding tiny bits to Zeal, who squealed with delight at his favourite parts of the movie as if he hadn't watched it over ten times already. The boy fell asleep halfway through and Abel tucked him in and read for about an hour before getting dressed. Philo came to fetch Zeal who woke as she lifted him.

'*Happy Feet!*' he cried as his gaze rested on his uncle. Then he closed his eyes and nodded off.

When Abel stopped to tell Ada he was meeting with Umannah, she didn't stir or ask questions like he would have, especially with the Santos problem still hanging.

'Take some money. Fifty, sixty thousand. Say it's to show appreciation for what they are doing,' she told him, not taking her eyes from the *Desperate Housewives* episode she was watching.

Umannah was early and already drinking a beer when Abel arrived at the restaurant.

'You got here before me.' Abel checked his time: it was still eight minutes before 2pm. He would have been there earlier if he hadn't stopped at an ATM to get the money Ada had suggested.

'Punctuality is the soul of business,' Umannah told him as they shook hands.

'Shall I order for us?'

'Yes, I am not used to fancy Chinese restaurants. Whatever is good for you is good for me.'

'It's a Thai restaurant,' Abel said before he could stop himself.

Umannah didn't seem to have noticed.

'We discovered movement on your brother's accounts,' he said when their starter arrived.

'Yes. We got a court injunction. The family was suffering. His business too.'

'And the new account that was opened in his company name with you and his wife as signatories?'

'We had to have money in an account we could access easily. It's an operations account, basically.'

The questions came and Abel answered, impressed that the police were, at least, as Nigerians like to say, doing something. They had polished off a bottle of red wine by the time the meal came to an end.

'The commissioner and DCP Balogun are on my case. They want answers and we have two weeks to deliver,' he told Abel. 'We have learnt quite a few things and I will discuss some with you next week before I submit my report.'

'That's good.' Abel reached into his jacket; the moment seemed right. 'I hope this doesn't offend you but I just wanted to show some appreciation for what you are doing for us.' He placed the envelope on the table.

'Oh, no offence taken.' Umannah palmed it and put it in his own jacket. 'As I told you, I knew your brother and he helped me once. I feel I have to pay him back,' Umannah said as he pushed back his chair and stood up.

'We will meet here, next week. I like their food. Classy. Money is good, my brother.' They shook hands. 'If I eat here with my own money, my wife and I will fight over chop money.'

Abel sat again after Umannah was gone. He had been scared but was now relieved that there had been no mention of Santos or Mayowa. As he waited for his bill, he considered what Ada had said about a permanent solution and shook his head. Santos was family; a blood relative. He had to find a way to sort that problem out in a way that was not *too* permanent.

—

Sunday crept by. Abel spent all of it upstairs, first in bed then watching movies with Ada. Neither of them bathed until evening.

They were overwhelmingly lethargic, as if the sleep they had been denied on Friday because of the night vigil had finally caught up with them.

Auntie Ekwi sent a mid-morning text on Monday: *I found a place in Ajegunle.*

Ajegunle! That was one place he had never been to in Lagos.

'It should be fine. I don't think it's as bad as it used to be,' Ada told him when he brought it up.

'Have you been there before?' he asked as they made a list of things to buy for the three days they would have to feed the twenty-one homeless children.

'No, but I have heard good things. Call Auntie Ekwi.'

'Is it not human beings who live there?' Auntie Ekwi fired back in Igbo. 'What is all this about? So living in Lekki has made you soft?'

Abel mumbled something and said he would call her back. She was obviously in a foul mood.

Ada called her later and they agreed to go to Ajegunle the next morning.

First they would visit the home they had been directed to. It was called Brothers' Keepers Foundation Home and run by a young woman. Auntie Ekwi had seen a story about the place in the papers.

'So you don't know her?' Ada asked.

'No, but it shouldn't be difficult. She takes care of the homeless: AIDS orphans, kids with different ailments – those who have been abandoned. She is always happy to get help.'

Ajegunle surprised Abel.

On the shift from the upscale locale of Apapa into Ajegunle, there appeared to be something like a time warp, as if one dimension had ceased to exist and another had taken its place.

He had expected a jungle but found an urban sprawl clawing at respectability. There were paved roads and multi-storeyed buildings. It was still a ghetto but one that was gradually and systematically shrugging off its past.

Their destination was called Dustbin Estate – a settlement, literarily on top of a refuse heap. They had to park and walk, and after a certain point the ground softened underfoot as if padded with sawdust.

But it wasn't the soft soil, the quasi-terra-firma that unnerved them; it was the unnerving stench. There was no reprieve, just a massive stink that hit you so hard you almost retched. Abel felt like the stench would never leave the soles of his shoes.

They found the home, which was no more than a rectangular structure built right by the canal. The floor was calcified refuse but the children sat on it as if on Persian rugs.

Stella Maris, the lady who had set up the place and now ran it, was all smiles as they explained that they had come to visit and feed the kids.

'God will bless you,' she kept saying as the children milled around, tugging at her frayed gown and pointing at the well-dressed strangers.

They had to see the Baale of Dustbin Estate, who was like some kind of overseer and chief, she told them, before they could drop off their gifts, since she and her foundation were there thanks to the magnanimity of the Baale and his community.

The Baale's house was a bungalow. He was sitting outside, smoking and drinking kai-kai, the local brew.

'Who be dis people?' he asked.

'Dem bring food come for our children,' she told him. He nodded and spat a glob of saliva into the gutter.

His house was different. Although built atop the refuse dump like the rest, he had paving stones on the floor. Still, there was no mistaking the fact that they were in Ajegunle. A thin rivulet of brackish green water ran from across the road to his verandah, before snaking its way under the house to the back where it met the canal. Every time the wind blew, the stench would waft up and foul the air.

The Baale asked a few questions and then Abel presented him with the Gordon's Gin and pack of cigarettes Stella Maris had asked them to buy.

'God go bless you people. Your children no go get wahala like these ones for here.' The Baale prayed as he set down the gifts and pocketed the ten thousand naira Abel had added.

Abel and Ada left Auntie Ekwi to handle the delivery and instructions. They also gave Stella Maris a cheque for two hundred thousand naira. Abel had wanted them to bring cash, but Ada had cautioned against it, saying she could be attacked and robbed once they left.

Stella Maris told him that she graduated from the University of Lagos with a 2.1 in economics and had been hoping to get a bank job until a story she read about a girl she knew changed her whole life. The girl had gotten pregnant, was thrown out of the house and found dead three months later, her breasts and private parts sliced off.

'I decided to do something for girls like her. So, I rented an apartment where I can house people in need. I set up that school with assistance from the Fountain of Life church so the children can, at least, learn to read and write.'

'How do you raise funds for this?' Ada asked her.

'Churches, some NGOs and kind-hearted people like you.'

Ada and Abel exchanged a glance. He made a mental note: when all this was over, he would make sure Stella Maris and the children under her care got something from them every month.

—

Bros, Iyawo is only a wife. Me and you are blood. Don't let her scatter our family.

He read the text again and again, glad to hear from Santos and happy that the tone had changed. He'd been amazed at Ada's rage and direct attack, but the more he thought about it the more he realised that that had been the best thing to do under the circumstances.

Santos had come ready and Abel had caved without a fight. It was Ada who saved the day. Both men were neck-deep in the Mayowa affair and if Santos squealed Ada suggested they turn the thing on him, get a good lawyer and see what happened.

He studied the text again and sent a reply: *Meet me at Terra Kulture. 2pm.*

'What are you going to tell him?' Ada asked.

He couldn't see her expression because a young lady was braiding her hair and her face was turned to the wall.

'Offer him twenty and ask him to leave Nigeria.'

'Leave Nigeria and go where?'

'Canada. He always dreamt about going abroad even as a child.'

'Visa?'

'I spoke to Nnamdi; he knows someone who can arrange it for a fee.'

'Guarantees?'

'Well, I am thinking of talking to Auntie Ekwi about it.'

'No, don't drag Auntie Ekwi into this.' Ada whirled round, pushing the girl away. 'Make Santos behave or I will fix him myself. I have suffered enough since Soni disappeared for anyone to stick his finger in my eyes. I can be respectful but I am never foolish.'

'Take it easy, Ada.'

She turned back to face the wall.

He drove to Terra Kulture, his mind in tumult. Could Santos be trusted? Would he accept twenty million naira and disappear? Should he up the figure? Give him something more substantial, something that could buy him a house in Canada? His mind was so pre-occupied he ran into a black Toyota Avensis as he turned into Ajose Adeogun.

'Oga, you no dey see?' the uniformed driver barked as Abel stepped out of the car.

He recalled immediately what Santos had told him once in traffic as they watched two men yell at each other after a fender bender: 'If you hit someone and you are driving the bigger car, don't step out. Make them come to you. If you stay in your car they will show you respect; if you step out they will insult you.'

'I beg your pardon, do you know who I am?' Abel snapped, surprising himself. 'Who do you work for? Don't you have manners? Is that how you talk to people?'

The driver took a closer look at Abel; the spanking white shirt, the black trousers, black leather shoes and gleaming BMW X5.

'Oga, my oga won't be happy with me,' he said, his tone now diffident and deferential.

Abel checked the damage. It wasn't much – a slight dent. 'Take it to the panel beater,' he ordered and handed him a wad of notes.

The man looked at the money, then up at Abel. He accepted it, bowed and drove off.

When Abel got into the car, his hands were shaking so badly he sat there and took his time calming down. *Do you know who I am?* He had asked the man the question he hated the most. And he was not sure he knew who he was or had become.

—

Santos seemed jumpy when Abel sat beside him.

'Bros, how far?'

Abel ignored him. 'I will buy a small house in your name in Canada and give you ten million naira. Total will be thirty million. I will help you get the visa and buy you a ticket. The day you step foot in Nigeria is the day you die. Send me a text if you accept my offer.'

Santos' mouth was still hanging open as Abel returned to his car. In the vehicle, he set his head upon the steering wheel and wept like a baby.

Back in Lekki, he crawled into the cloying darkness under the duvet, the air conditioner on full blast. He wanted to crawl deeper and deeper, to be swallowed whole, to disappear and forget it all. Three months, and everything had changed. He had crossed some invisible line and become someone he could not even recognise. There was blood on his hands and lust on his mind. He had assumed another man's wealth; how could he not be affected?

Days ago, he was being choked by the stench of filth in Dustbin Estate; now it was his descent into Hades occupying his thoughts. His life was gradually becoming a mad dash from things he couldn't handle. When the running would end, he had no idea. But while he still had some control, Abel wanted to keep fighting this thing taking him over like a body-devouring virus.

He cried, stopped and cried again. He wished he had never received that text message, that Soni had never been abducted, that the papers hadn't gotten wind of the story, that he had never agreed to go along with Santos and make Mayowa 'vomit that money'. He was tainted, a man for whom redemption lay only in the impossibility of retracing his steps.

He remembered the day his father died and the stranger who had come to tell him.

'I have some bad news.' The man had made him leave halfway through his lecture. 'There has been a death in the family. Your father was shot two days ago.'

Abel had staggered, stunned, as if the news was a physical blow. The man reached out a hand to steady him. He said his thanks, ashamed of the fact that when the man said there had been a death in the family, his first thought had been of his mother. Later, long after he had cried and been consoled by Calista, he was finally able to appreciate the irony of the situation. He was the one for whom everyone was on an unending vigil and here he was getting ready to bury his father.

'It was a policeman in Benin,' his sister told him days later, when he got home. She had been in the car when it happened. 'We were going to See Uncle Benny. The policeman was clearly drunk and he wouldn't let us drive through even though the car in front had just been let through after the driver gave him a tip. Daddy had also been drinking but that day it was as if Daddy wanted the man to shoot him. Daddy said, "No, I must drive through and I won't give you a farthing." But the man would not listen; he just kept telling Daddy to reverse. When Daddy refused, he started deflating the tyres. That was when Daddy came down from the car. Mummy was screaming as Daddy went to stop the policeman. Daddy pushed him away and the man just turned, pointed his gun and shot Daddy in the stomach. Twice. Then he ran.'

Their mother would never discuss it, not then, not ever.

When Abel found Soni and told him, his brother had run off screaming 'NO' over and over again, as if the policeman who had shot and killed their father was hot on his heels. They would drag him back to the room many hours later in a drunken stupor.

It was in Calista that Abel had sought comfort and lying there in the darkness under the duvet he wished he could call her and unburden his heart to her one more time but this was one secret he could not share.

—

The church was full. Abel and Ada had had some trouble finding a spot to park and every available space had been taken up inside too.

'It's a special service,' Auntie Ekwi told them, clearly elated. 'It happens once a quarter.'

The Prophet was in his element. He danced, he pranced around, he spoke in tongues and anointed members of the congregation with oil, many of them falling under the anointing.

This time, the night seemed shorter, as if familiarity made the hours speed by.

Just before 5am, the Prophet stood at the front of the church and waited for the congregation to file past. A young man was holding up a bowl of anointing oil and the Prophet would dip into the bowl and slap his open palm on the congregant's forehead, smearing them with oil as he screamed 'Take it, my son' or 'Take it, my daughter'.

The congregation went round and round until it got to a woman kneeling in prayer at the back. Those around had let her be, but when the crowd thinned an usher went to prod her. The kneeling woman keeled over; she had died on her knees.

Everyone ran.

SOMEBODY REMOVED THE LADDER

DSP Umannah was looking sharp that Saturday and by the time Abel got to the restaurant, he was halfway through a bottle of red wine.

'This wine is good,' he told Abel as they shook hands. 'I remembered it from last week,'

'Yes. I remember it too.' Something made him feel that Umannah had purposely arrived early on account of that wine.

'So, you said your report is done and you have news for me,' Abel said as soon as he had placed their order.

'Yes. I have finished my report and will submit it on Monday. There are things I felt I should discuss with you, seeing that we have become quite acquainted and because your brother was good to me.'

'Sure.' Abel's palms were clammy from anxiety. 'What have you found out?'

'When I read Ofio's report, I had the sense that he did a good job, which is why I have merged our two reports into one. This case was reassigned to me because, in the past three years, my team and I have cracked four missing people's cases. I will be straight with you, and this is off the record. This is what a friend will do for another. I have reasons to believe your brother was a victim of criminal rivalry.' His eyes bored straight into Abel's.

'This is not the kind of report we give to family members, but your brother was good to me and you have been good to me. When this case started everyone was a suspect from Santos to his wife, but gradually people were eliminated.' He paused to take a sip. 'I am sure you know the kind of business your brother was into, right?' Abel nodded. 'It was high yield, high risk. There was a lot of money involved. Someone got greedy, others got pissed off and your brother disappeared. We will keep looking but I can almost tell you with certainty that he will never be found.' He paused, but when Abel did not react, he went ahead.

'I am sorry, Abel, but these kinds of people don't bury bodies or make ransom demands. They simply disappear you to teach others a lesson. I am really sorry but that's the case we have here.'

Abel was silent for a long time. It was one thing to have a hunch, but a completely different ball game when you knew for certain. Here was a policeman telling him that his younger brother, a man who had a wife and a son, was gone forever. How did you digest or communicate that piece of news? How would he tell their mother?

'I am really sorry Abel. I wish I had better news than this. The commissioner has requested a report and this will be my summation. But I suppose the family needs closure so I will ask you to go see this man.' He pushed a piece of paper at Abel. 'Call him and say you are from me. He is expecting you.'

Abel took the paper. On it was the name 'Walata' – a nickname, he was sure – and a phone number.

'Today?'

'Yes, today. He lives in Ikoyi.'

Abel thanked him and rose. 'I will take care of the bill.'

Outside, Abel nosed the car out of Musa Yar'adua Street, drove down Idowu Taylor to Adeola Odeku and onto Ahmadu Bello. He was in Ikoyi ten minutes later, something that would never be possible on a weekday. As he drove into Osborne, he dialled Walata's number, praying he would be home.

'Who give you this number?'

'DSP Umannah.'

'About Sabato?'

'Yes.'

'I will text you my address. I am waiting.'

The house was on Lugard Avenue, a few hundred metres from the UNICEF office. The road was bad, waterlogged and filled with potholes. Abel's car got snagged and he had to rev and reverse before he could continue.

Walata was bare-chested. Tall, dark and imposing, he had a deep voice and cut the picture of a criminal who had managed the tricky transition from the mainland into the gentrified locale of old Ikoyi.

His house was an all-white duplex that sat on huge grounds. There wasn't much free space inside: big ceramic vases stood all over the house like sentries guarding the paintings and sculptures, most of them by stars and masters of contemporary Nigerian art.

Abel looked around while Walata took a call. He espied an Enwonwu, a Grillo, an Onobrakpeya and two by El Anatsui. There were paintings from Gani Odutokun, Ndidi Dike, Rom Isichei, Kanebi Osanebi, Victor Ehikhamenor, Uche Edochie and others whose signatures he couldn't read.

'You really like art,' Abel said when Walata finished his call.

'They are investments.' His voice was gruff, his English flailing as he explained what he meant. 'A white man tell me once, art works can be a store of value. I don't know who the artists are but I get this Lebanese woman who help me to buy and she say if I ever need money she can help me sell. And she say, if the artist die I will get more money. So, maybe if I need money and I want to sell something, I will kill the artist first.' Abel began to laugh before he realised the man wasn't joking.

'Let's go to the garden. What do you want to drink? I have single malt whisky. Glenlivet. Very nice. Hot drink that feel like ice cream in your mouth.'

Abel accepted the drink. He set it down on the table and waited for Walata to drink before he followed suit. The drink was smooth, going down with the slightest burn. The brute was right – a hot drink that felt like ice cream.

'I know your brother well. I work with Sabato Rabato. We make money together. He is a good guy but he have one problem.' Walata said as he refilled his glass.

Sitting down, his huge belly hung in massive folds. He had three tattoos, one on each bicep and another on his chest. The one on his chest was in old text and, sitting close, Abel eventually made out the word 'ekun'.

Yoruba for 'tiger'.

'See, I tell you we have made money. Plenty. But there is one thing I can never forget: everybody must bow to somebody. Pope bow to Jesus, Jesus bow to God, even Devil sef, bow to God. But Sabato don't believe in that kind of thing. He used to call himself a self-made man, but I don't think so. You cannot make yourself. After God has created us somebody will make us. There is difference between creating and making, I tell you.'

He paused to take a call, during which he issued threats. Abel shuddered: the way Walata sounded on the phone was the way he must have sounded to Santos.

Walata took a sip, smacked his lips and turned back to Abel. 'See, this is how I see life. Everybody need ladder to climb up and sometimes that ladder is a human being. You understand?' Abel nodded. 'So, that is what happened to Sabato. I think after he climb up somebody remove the ladder.'

Abel inhaled deeply and let it out slowly.

Here he was drinking, without doubt, the best Scotch he had ever tasted, with a rich thug who may have killed his brother, or given the order, and he was powerless to do anything.

Steeling himself, he downed the drink in his glass and rose to his feet.

'Walata, tell me, did you kill my brother?'

'Me?' He looked insulted. 'My brother, I have done many, many bad things in my life but Sabato was my friend. He was foolish and stubborn but he was my friend. But you see, in this world there is nobody you like more than yourself. I did not kill Sabato, but I did not stop them from removing the ladder.'

He rose to his full height, dwarfing Abel.

'This is Lagos, my brother and good and bad things happen at once.'

———

Abel cried all the way home, the tears streaming down his face as he drove. From the moment he got the text that morning in Asaba, he had known this wasn't going to end well, yet that could not lessen the blow from Walata. As the man led him to the gate of his huge property, Abel had asked him one last question.

'Do you know who removed the ladder?'

There was a long pause. Walata tapped him on the shoulder and said, 'My brother, this thing we do is like war. When a soldier fall down in the war front, how can you know which of the bullet killed him?'

Abel's tears were for their mother, their sister Oby, for Ada and for Zeal. He cried for himself, for the brother he hadn't really known, for the love he didn't fully acknowledge.

He tried to remember the last time he had seen Soni. It was about eight months before he disappeared. Soni had dropped by to see him at school. Abel was supervising a continuous assessment test and had only had time for a handshake before Soni left with his friends to Enugu State where a business partner was getting married.

Abel wished he had had more time, and that instead of a handshake he had given his brother a hug. It was those fleeting goodbyes that haunted you, those half-realised farewells that remained forever in abeyance.

—

Later that night, many hours after he had returned, the harbinger of bad tidings, he lay in bed, cowering under the duvet as he listened to her sobs. When he could take it no longer, he turned the key and opened the door that connected their rooms.

She was kneeling at her bed as if she had been praying, naked from the waist up, her gown bunched around her.

'It's OK,' he said pulling her up and enfolding her in his embrace, her breasts against his bare chest.

He was aroused and knew she could feel his erection now. He held her, both of them half-naked on that bed for what seemed like a long time. Then she looked up with tear-filled eyes and kissed him. He tasted salt and wine and desire. He pushed her back on her bed and took one hard, dark nipple in his mouth. Ada cried out as if in pain but when he made to pull away she pushed his head back.

He covered her body with kisses, from her face and her neck down to her belly, luxuriating in the essence of that which he had imagined for so long. When he pulled down her dress, he was surprised to see that she wore no panties.

He kissed between her legs, tongue flicking over pubis, lips over labia, tasting her and teasing out moans as she pulled her dress over her head and flung it across the room. She reached out and pulled off his boxers.

They didn't fall asleep afterwards. They just talked, her fingers tracing the welts on his back where she had dug in and drawn blood as she climaxed not once, not twice, but thrice.

She talked about the night she met Soni at the club. He had been confident, in control, without an iota of shyness. She talked about the first time they made love, how he had triggered her first multiple orgasms. She told him about finding his letter and hating him. She spoke about the wedding, how she tried to see what it was that made Soni think Abel was the salt of the earth.

'Don't you feel oppressed by this constant urge to be good?' she asked him.

'I am not always good,' he said, kissing her lightly. 'I just have a low threshold for trouble.'

She told him again about refusing to name her son after him and the big fight that had caused between her and Soni. She told him about the day Soni disappeared.

'We had been fighting and I wasn't speaking to him.' A month before, he had come back after a trip abroad and when she unpacked his things she found a pair of panties in his bag. 'They'd been worn, stained.' The pain was raw in her voice. 'We hadn't made love in one month and I just lost it. I didn't let him touch me. By the time he disappeared, we hadn't made love for two months. I was tired. I knew I wanted him but I felt betrayed. See, I always knew there would be other women. He told me before we got married and I accepted that. My friends couldn't get it but I used to put condoms in his bag when he was travelling. I knew I couldn't stop him so I had to keep himself and myself protected.'

Ada reached over and picked up the remote control to turn off the air conditioner.

'It's too cold,' she said, snuggling up to him. 'I couldn't go to another man. That's not me. Despite all his women, I knew Soni loved me and would die for me. So I stayed faithful. I had planned a wild night that Saturday evening. I bought edible undies. I did my hair. I cooked a nice meal. I changed his sheets, lit scented candles and sent him a naughty text like I used to. He replied *Can't wait my love. See you at 9pm.*

'But 9pm came and he didn't come home. I thought, Lagos traffic, but by 9.30 I was getting worried. I called his number; it rang once then went off. I called Santos, who said Soni had told him to take the day off so he wasn't with him. I didn't sleep. The candles burnt out. The food went cold. I called his friends and people he did business with. No one had seen him.

Santos and I went to the police the next day. They said we had to wait for seventy-two hours. Or was it forty-eight? I told them it was unusual. Soni could be crazy but he was never irresponsible. The police asked if we'd been fighting, if there was another woman. I told him we just made up, and one of them sniggered. "Maybe oga hasn't made up with you," he said. I told him to shut it. The other officer apologised.'

They called her two days later to say she should come and identify a car that had been found in a ditch.

'I told them it was Soni's car and they said, "Well, that is cause for some happiness. There was no blood, no gunshots, and no damage. So, we believe he left the car alive." That was almost four months ago, Abel.' She eased up on an elbow to look at him. 'I pray every day but I am all prayed out. I know what Soni did for a living, the women he slept with and the kind of men he dealt with. I knew something like this could happen and with so much time gone, I have no reason to believe he will come out of this alive. I have lost all hope.'

When she paused to turn the AC back on, Abel leaned close and flicked a tongue over her nipple.

'And you haven't helped matters,' she said, pushing him away playfully. 'I have been on fire since you came into this house. When I walk past you or touch you I want to catch alight. The only time I felt like that was with Soni.'

Abel hushed her with a kiss and pulled her to himself. He held her close as they both cried and fell asleep.

—

Abel wakes up sweating. The luminous dial of the clock on Ada's wall tells him it is seven minutes past 3am. That is when he realises, or rather, finally admits to himself, that he does not want Soni to be found. Not now. Not ever.

He looks at Soni's wife sleeping half-naked beside him and realises that, like fingers in a glove, he has found his niche.

Lagos is now his home.

THE END